$200 GIRL

She called herself Penny—but it took four crisp fifties to buy her for a weekend.

I had the money—and so I had Penny. When I handed over her fee, Penny was in trouble. One thing she didn't know about her new customer—

I was the Assistant D. A. in charge of smashing the vicious call-girl ring!

MARINO AND MACAULEY

Nick Marino is a pen name hiding
the identity of a top-ranking author
who has scored many outstanding literary
successes. In ONE WAY STREET
he introduced

Mike Macauley, the tough young Assistant
D. A., who's as fast with a girl as he
is with a gun. CITY LIMITS brings Mike
back in his deadliest—and most
femme-filled—case.

CITY LIMITS

by **WILL OURSLER**
writing as Nick Marino

WILDSIDE PRESS

CITY LIMITS

chapter one

WHEN I GOT THERE, the defendant had already taken her place on a high-backed wooden chair with the rays of the first really hot June sun of the year slanting down on her through the big open window and the courtroom dust like a spotlight.

She was good-looking, and that surprised me. She had tawny hair worn longer than you usually see it these days, and she had skin which would tan a deep bronze during the summer, if she didn't spend the summer months acquiring a prison pallor. She didn't look the type who would be sitting with a brawny policewoman behind her, facing a morals charge.

The judge nodded his head a half inch to show he had seen me come in. If he thought it peculiar that an assistant D.A. wanted to sit in on a prostitution case in Women's Court, he hadn't said anything when I called and asked for permission to be there.

The cop who was testifying wore plain clothes. He wasn't looking at the woman and she wasn't looking at him. He was saying in a steady, unhurried and unhappy voice, "So I came down Washington Street—"

"Walking?" the judge asked.

"Walking, your honor. The defendant was standing there, window shopping. She must have seen my reflection in the window. She turned around and smiled. I stopped a little ways off and straightened my tie. She smiled again and came over to me and we both smiled. Then we started in talking."

"Did she proposition you?" the judge asked.

"Not right away, your honor. I asked if she wanted something and she said what did I think, and before you know it we walk over to Melville Avenue, where she's got an apartment."

"What does 'before you know it' consist of?"

"Just small talk, your honor. I don't remember it very well. Anyhow, we went over to her place and she told me it would be twenty-five dollars, which I gave her." The plain clothes man's voice became so faint, the judge had to tell him to speak more distinctly. He said, "Then she undressed and I told her she was under arrest."

The judge leaned forward to look down at the woman. "Does the defendant wish to speak?"

"No, your honor," the woman said in a small voice.

I raised my eyes to the bench and the judge said, "Assistant District Attorney Macauley, I believe, has something to say which may be relevant here before sentence is passed. Mr. Macauley?"

I stepped forward while everyone, including the testifying plain clothes man, whom I knew personally, looked surprised. My job in an understaffed D.A.'s office was no cinch, but I wouldn't have traded places with that plain clothes man for a million bucks, tax free. He was a member of the Morals Division, which meant that he spent his time playing the part of a visiting fireman who got himself picked up by prostitutes, propositioned by pimps and sometimes by dope pushers. For this he got exactly what the patrolman on the beat got, eighty-five bucks a week in his pay envelope, and something the beat cop never got at all—a hard, cynical attitude toward the world. He could have it.

I said, "I'd like to ask the defendant a few questions, your honor."

"You have the court's permission."

I turned to the woman. This close, she was hardly more than a girl. She wore a spring-weight suit, and it was too hot in the courtroom for that kind of clothing. A fine dew of perspiration beaded her forehead and her upper lip, but her face was under perfect control. She had spent a few days in the common jail, and wore no makeup. She looked pale, but you could tell that with a little makeup, or maybe just some fresh air, she would be a knockout.

"Your name is Gloria Townsend?" I asked her.

"Yes."

"Did you phone the district attorney's office on last May twenty-third?"

"No."

"You're testifying under oath."

She hesitated. "I don't remember if I called or not."

"Do you remember talking to me? Macauley's the name."

"I don't remember talking to anybody."

I frowned at her. "About the call-girl racket in this city?" I prompted.

"I don't know anything about a call-girl racket." She jerked her head in the plain clothes man's direction. "He picked me up for a streetwalker."

The judge and I exchanged glances. I said a little desperately, "You told me you were fed up with the life you led. You told me you wanted out. You told me—"

She interrupted. "How could I have told you anything, if I don't remember talking to you?"

The brawny policewoman tried to hide a smile. The judge cleared his throat and said, "Mr. Macauley, much as this court would like to help you, if the defendant maintains that position, I'm afraid your line of questioning is pointless."

He was right, of course. I nodded and apologized to the court for wasting its time.

Gloria Townsend sat with her hands in her lap, studying her fingernails. The plain clothes man, Harry Allerup, was looking down at the floor. I decided to hang around while the court passed sentence, although I knew what the stenence would be.

The court officer came up and read Gloria Townsend's health report. She had passed with flying colors. He informed the judge that the defendant had no previous record, and that her permanent address was listed as c/o Smith, R.F.D. Two. R.F.D. Two was about twelve miles outside the city limits along the river road.

"R.F.D. Two!" I blurted. "Don't you get it, your honor? That's the old Rivershore Drive outside the city. Headquarters for the call-girl racket which—"

"Mr. Macauley," the judge said slowly, in the same tone he would probably use to scold his grandchild, "the alleged racket has no bearing on this case, and this court has no jurisdiction on Rivershore Drive." He smiled at me, though, sympathetically. It was no secret that the city's call-girl racket had been dumped in my lap by the D.A. as a kind of extracurricular activity. That was six months ago, and I'd been banging my head against a stone wall ever since, until Gloria Townsend's call. Now Gloria had changed her mind and I was back at my same old spot against the wall, only now the wall was harder.

The judge cleared his throat and sentenced Gloria Townsend to six months in the workhouse, then suspended sentence because the girl had no previous record. The police-woman nudged Gloria and said, "Well, you're free."

"Am I?"

"Yes, dearie."

Gloria got up. She was a tall girl and carried herself well. The other plain clothes men sitting on the long wooden bench, waiting unhappily for their turns to testify against the other prostitutes who would parade through Women's Court this morning, never took their eyes off her.

"I won't be long," Gloria Townsend said.

"You won't be what?" the policewoman asked her. They came slowly toward where I was standing, between Harry Allerup and the police bench.

"Long," said Gloria Townsend, and walked over to plain clothes man Allerup and smiled at him. Harry Allerup smiled back. It was a surprised and timid smile.

Gloria made a noise in her throat, her face worked con-vulsively and she spit in Allerup's face.

The brawny policewoman grabbed Gloria's arms and twisted them behind her until the girl winced. Allerup wiped his face with his display handkerchief as Gloria turned to look defiantly at the judge.

The judge glared at her. "There will be an additional thirty days for contempt of court."

Gloria looked indifferent.

"Suspended," said the judge bitterly, bleakly. The work-house, women's division, was overcrowded. The order was to get them back on the street, where they'd be better off than sharing overcrowded prison accommodations with the really bad ones. You couldn't blame the prison officials.

The matron and Gloria Townsend went outside. I followed them into the corridor and hurried to make the elevator just as they got on. I stood in front of Gloria with my back to the door and looked at her steadily.

"I don't have to talk to you," she said.

"Why'd you change your mind?"

"Do I have to talk to him?" she asked the matron.

"No, dearie. You're free. I'm only taking you downstairs to get your things."

"What I can't figure," I said suddenly, getting close to Gloria Townsend and looking at her eyes while I spoke, "is why a high-class call girl like you takes up streetwalking in her spare time. Hobby?"

"Ah, what's the use?" Gloria said. "You cops are all the same." She said it with such depths of bitterness, even the impassive Negro elevator operator turned around and stared at her.

She turned away and faced a rear corner of the elevator. Her shoulders began to move, and by the time we reached the street floor her whole body was shaking with sobs.

The elevator door opened. A small crowd of people waited politely for us to get out before they got on. Nobody moved.

Then Gloria Townsend turned around and said very softly, "That son-of-a-bitch. That no-good, lying son-of-a-bitch." She said it devoutly, almost as if she were praying.

"Who?" I asked "Allerup?"

She hit me on the face with her left hand. She was going to use her right hand too, but the matron picked that one off in the air and held it. They walked past me and out of the elevator. The matron gave me one of those looks only two-hundred-pound policewomen can give. Men, the look said, every one of you. It said a lot of other things, but they aren't printable.

The crowd filing into the elevator tried to duplicate that look. They couldn't, but it was still one hell of a way to start the morning.

chapter two

"WHY DON'T YOU get wise to yourself, Mike, and lay off?" District Attorney William P. ("Sunshine") Sever asked me.

The nickname fitted him, for he was the original jolly fat man, when he wanted to be. All two hundred and fifty pounds of him. He could beam a smile at you like a ray of sunshine. He was a politician's dream as a district attorney. A reasonably honest politician's dream. Because Sunshine Sever was an honest D.A.—to a point—but also knew that politics did indeed make strange bed-fellows and that a D.A.'s job is basically political.

"Lay off?" I asked. "I sent for Allerup because I wanted to talk to him. What's wrong with that?"

"I'll tell you what's wrong," Sunshine said, depositing his big rump on a corner of my desk and hitching his belt up with oddly slender, almost dainty thumbs. "But it won't do one hell of a bit of good, will it?"

"You haven't told me yet," I said.

"This city has a good Morals Division, Mike," Sunshine said slowly. "I don't have to tell you what kind of help it can be to this office. So far we've gotten along great with Lieutenant Spooner. Just great, Mike. I'd hate to see our relationship with the division loused up."

"Who's lousing it up? I don't have anything against Lieutenant Spooner. I don't even have anything against Harry Allerup. I only want to ask him a few questions. I'm going to, Sunshine."

"Damn it, I know you are. But hell, Mike, use your head. Allerup testified in court, didn't he? Are you going to tell me you don't believe his sworn testimony?"

I got tired of arguing. A little coldly I said, "I'll put it this way, Sunshine. Either I question Harry Allerup the way I want to, or I'll toss the whole call-girl business back in your lap."

"Now, Mike," he said, his voice holding a mixture of reproachfulness and paternal pain. He didn't like the choice, because he really didn't have any. The Citizens' Committee for Good Government and a runaway grand jury had dumped the call-girl problem in Sunshine's ample lap originally when a call girl named Mona St. Clair had taken an overdose of sleeping pills and died. I'd taken it on as extra duty after Sunshine had practically gotten down on his knees and begged me.

"Listen," I said. "Gloria Townsend phones and says she's fed up with going on two-hundred-buck weekends with clammy-handed sugar daddies. She's willing to tell everything she knows about the call-girl racket. Then what happens?"

"You already told me what happened," Sunshine groaned.

"Allerup picks her up on a morals charge," I said, ignoring him. "And she promptly forgets she ever spoke to me. Does it figure? After the trial she spits in his face and later, in the elevator, calls him a lying so-and-so. When I say, 'Who? Allerup?' she hauls off and slugs me. You figure it out, chief."

"I don't want to figure it out."

"I'm saying she knows Allerup better than came out at her trial. I'm saying—"

"Mike," Sunshine groaned. He really looked miserable.

"Well, you can stick around while I ask him."

"That's white of you," he said. "You're not going to fire me, huh?"

Before I could answer this bit of sarcasm, the office PBX buzzed and I flicked the little button with my thumb. Miss Rains' voice said, "Detective Allerup to see you, Mike."

I looked at Sunshine. "I'll stay," Sunshine said.

"Send him in," I told Miss Rains, and a moment later Detective Harry Allerup entered my sanctum sanctorum.

Harry Allerup was a tall, good-looking guy on the right side of thirty by three or four years. He wore tweeds, and a plain clothes man in tweeds is about as common as a D.A. in tights. He smiled at Sunshine and I introduced them and watched them shake hands. The District Attorney has a grip like a wood vise, but Allerup didn't wince. He said, "You wanted to see me, Mr. Macauley?"

The Mr. Macauley got me. I'd known Harry Allerup ever since he'd made the Morals Division, and it had been Harry and Mike ever since, for more than a year.

"Yeah," I said. "I wanted to see you—Detective Allerup."

We looked at each other. I smiled first, then Harry Allerup grinned at me. He still looked uneasy, though. "Aw, Mike," he said.

"Sit down, Harry," I said.

He took a seat. "Lieutenant Spooner says I'm to coöperate in every way possible," he said stiffly.

"There, you see?" Sunshine boomed at me.

"That's what Lieutenant Spooner said, Harry. What do you say?"

"I don't even know what you wanted to see me about, Mike."

Before I could tell him, the PBX buzzed again. Pushing down the button, I started to say, "I don't want to be dis—"

Miss Rains broke in excitedly, "Remember when you came back from the Courts Building yesterday morning and said if a Miss Gloria Townsend got in touch with this office I was to drop whatever I was doing and—"

"Gloria Townsend!" I shouted.

Harry Allerup stiffened in his chair as though it were a trial run for the hot seat. Sunshine looked like Sunshine will look when he's dismayed.

"On the telephone, Mike," Miss Rains said.

I pushed the switch over to one of the outside lines before she could tell me which number. I got a dial tone for my trouble. I pushed the switch again, and this time there was the faint sound of music. Otherwise silence.

"Macauley," I said.

I didn't recognize her voice over the telephone. She sounded somehow more sure of herself, as though she could do what had to be done as long as she didn't have to look the world squarely in the eye. "This is Gloria Townsend, Mr. Macauley. I—I did a lot of thinking last night and I—"

Her voice trailed off and the background music seemed to rise in volume. I shouted, "Are you still there? Where are you?"

"It's hot in this phone booth," Gloria Townsend said. "They ought to have a fan. I want to see you, Mr. Macauley."

"Right now," I said. "Wherever you are. Don't go away."

"I won't, Mr. Macauley. It's a roadhouse on Rivershore Drive. The Lagoon. You know the place?"

"I can find it," I said. "I'm on my way."

I cut the connection and got my Panama and told Sunshine, "She's in a place called the Lagoon on Rivershore. I'm going out there."

"Rivershore is outside our jurisdiction, Mike."

"I'm just going to talk to the dame," I said hotly. "What do I need, a volunteer deputy sheriff's badge?"

"Take it easy, Mike."

Instead of answering him, I asked Allerup, "Want to come along for the ride?"

"No thanks, Mike. I'd rather not."

"Don't want to see her, huh?"

"What's that supposed to mean?" Allerup demanded, flushing.

I looked at him. "You tell me, Harry. I'll listen all the way out to Rivershore."

"No. You saw what she thought of me."

"What do you care? You're a cop, aren't you?"

"Aw, go to hell," he said, and stormed out of the office. I tried to swap glances with Sunshine, but he wasn't

trading. I went outside and Miss Rains pointed to the door.
"He went thataway," she said.

There wasn't any other way to go. I said, "I thought
maybe he jumped out the window."

When I reached the corridor, the elevator doors were
already sliding shut. I shrugged and took the steps down
the five flights to the basement garage and drew an official
black Merc from the City Hall car pool. The dispatcher
asked if I wanted a driver, and I said I did not. I felt an
urgency tugging at my muscles, constricting my throat and
making it dry. I didn't know why, but I knew I was going
to hurry.

I took City Hall Street to Mark Twain Boulevard, running two traffic lights before I decided to switch on the
siren. After that it was smooth sailing out Mark Twain
to the Hawkins Creek Bridge and across the Bridge to
Rivershore Drive. Suburban housing developments slipped
by and a billboard told me what kind of gasoline was best
for my car. I looked at the speedometer. I was doing seventy-five and the needle was climbing.

The suburbs gave way to farmland and more billboards.
At a crossroad a state cop in gray uniform kicked over
his motorcycle and came after me. I had cut the siren after
crossing the Hawkins Creek Bridge, but I switched it back
on and the state cop pulled back and out of sight. He didn't
have to; I guess it was professional courtesy.

I was just congratulating myself on the good time I was
making when the left rear tire blew with a sound like a
.45 fired in a small room without any windows.

chapter three

THE MERC SWERVED WILDLY out of control. I kept my foot
on the gas pedal, as they tell you to in the auto-club safety
booklets, and began to fight the wheel for my life.

The Merc went into a long, smooth skid toward the
wrong side of the road as a big semi-trailer barrelled up
toward it. I threw the wheel in the direction of the skid

and we kept on going across Rivershore Drive to the opposite shoulder, where the Merc shuddered and spun in a full circle before it skidded back on the asphalt half a dozen feet behind the semi-trailer, went up on two wheels and almost over on its side, then came down hard with a jolt that probably ruined both the springs and my digestion.

After that I guided her over to the right-hand shoulder and got out, running around to the back and opening the trunk. In another minute I had the car up on its jack and looked at the damage. There was a hole in the tire Nashua could have run through. The tube was completely gone. I got out the spare and the lug wrench and went to work.

When I finished I was sweating. The whole thing hadn't taken fifteen minutes, but it was a hot day, the second really hot one of the summer. Besides, I was still anxious about Gloria Townsend.

Motorists went by, showing me their dust. The sky was blue and absolutely clear. It would have been a fine day for a dip in the Missouri, along which Rivershore Drive runs.

I climbed back into the Merc, lighted a cigarette with the dash lighter and wished I'd brought my pipe along after the first acrid puff. When the paper stuck to my fingers wetly, I got rid of the cigarette and pressed the starter button.

It ground and ground, but the motor didn't catch. I glanced at the temperature gauge. It was way over in the red. The hot day, the fast drive out here and fifteen minutes of standing under the hot sun had overheated the car.

I cursed and went around front and lifted the hood. I looked at my wristwatch. Gloria Townsend had called me over forty minutes ago. I wondered if she would still be waiting, then went back behind the wheel and tried the starter button once more. No soap.

I went out on the road and lifted my thumb. The motorists showed me more dust. Lots more dust. The official shield was on the wrong side of the Merc. I glared at the sun, and it glared back down at me. I was strictly an amateur. I got back inside the car and waited.

Ten minutes dragged by, showing their rear ends reluctantly, or maybe provocatively, like can-can dancers, before I was able to kick the overheated engine over. My rear tires threw gravel like a dog pawing dirt as I spun the car back on the asphalt and pushed the gas pedal to the floorboards.

A motor court flashed by on the left, and an army of billboards on the right. There was a drive-in theater and then two roadhouses, each with a handful of cars parked outside. It was mid-morning, after the breakfast rush and before the early lunchers would arrive. The two roadhouses looked lonely.

The third one did not. The third one, coming up swiftly on my left, was the Lagoon.

A dozen or more cars were in the small parking lot as I swung across the road. Two of them were blue Fords with the county sheriff's shield on them. A sheriff's deputy trying to look tough under his low-crowned Stetson, but managing only to look nasty, kept a growing mob of people away from the Lagoon's double door.

I hit the gravel of the parking lot on the run and elbowed my way into the crowd. "What's going on?" I asked the deputy.

"Nothing in it for you, mister."

I took out my wallet and let him look at what was behind the plastic window.

"Assistant D.A., huh? Well, I dunno. This ain't the city."

The crowd was quiet now. This was official talk and they wanted to hear it.

"Do you get out of the way, or do I have to walk over you?" I asked quietly.

A pink hand jerked the brim of the Stetson up. It was a western hat and a western gesture, but this wasn't the west. The deputy looked me up and down and said, "Aw, shoot, you can go in there, I reckon."

I said, "Thanks, podner," and did so. Someone in the crowd tittered, and the deputy was looking nasty again as I went by. For a minute there he had looked just plain scared.

It was dimly lit inside the Lagoon, but not cool. The dry heat of outdoors was replaced by a damp, sodden, beer-smelling wet heat.

"D.A.'s office," I said to one of the waiters lounging around uneasily. "What's the trouble?"

He jerked a thumb. "Sheriff's back there, mister."

I went the way he had pointed. At first I didn't get it. There was a bar on one side and some booths on the other, all of them empty. Beyond them in one direction was the door to the kitchen. Nearby a jukebox wanted to know why I didn't love it. A second sheriff's deputy was leaning against the jukebox, polishing his star with the lapel of his seersucker jacket. He was hatless and balding. Beyond him was a little alcove with two doors marked "Boys" and "Girls."

"You want what?" the deputy said.

"What happened to the people who were here?"

"Before the beating you mean? Who're you, Ace?"

"D.A.'s office," I said. "I was to meet a Miss Townsend here."

He shook his balding head. "Only one or two customers. Yeah, two of 'em. They're out front with the waiters. Both men." Then he shifted his weight forward away from the jukebox and said, "Holy Jesus, did you say Townsend?"

A lump of ice formed in the pit of my stomach. A blow-out, I thought irrelevantly, irrationally. You had to go and have a blowout.

The deputy went down the little hall to the door marked "Girls" and poked his head in to say, "Guy out here wantsta see Miss Townsend. Says he's from the D.A.'s office."

He listened for a moment with his head out of sight beyond the door, then came back to me and said, "You claim you're from the D.A. Now convince me."

I showed him my wallet and he pointed like a hunting dog, with his face, toward the door he had just left. I went back there and then turned around and looked at him. He nodded and gave me a lewd grin to take in with me. I opened the door and went in.

The walls were white-tiled and bounced back the reflection of a fluorescent ceiling light. There were two private cubicles, closed, and two sinks with a long mirror over both. There was one of those electronic drying gadgets. There was a strong disinfectant smell. There was another door, beyond the sinks, leading outside, probably to the parking lot. My guess was the sheriff had locked it, because it was closed and locked.

The sheriff watched me come in. I had met him once or twice when our paths crossed officially, but we were bare acquaintances. His name was Merz and he was a big man with a lot of once-solid beef going soft as he approached middle age ungracefully. He was hatless and wore what looked like a faded denim work shirt, open at the collar to reveal matted graying hair. There were tufts of hair protruding from his nostrils and other tufts in his ears. There seemed to be an overabundance of hair everywhere except on his head, which sported a scant fringe around back between the ears. His eyes were as expressive as the reverse sides of campaign buttons.

He said, "This the lady you're looking for?"

She was on the floor between the sinks and the closed cubicles. Her knees were up and her skirt had slid over her thighs almost to her waist. Her shoes were off and one of them was in the sink, the high heel twisted and broken. She had been beaten with them brutally.

Her legs were black and blue. The summery print dress she wore was torn from neckline to belt down one side. The elastic strap of her bra had torn too, or the snap had parted, exposing the untouched white and pink of her right breast. It was the only untouched part of her I could see. Even her face was battered and swollen beyond recognition. I recognized her by the long, beautiful tawny hair.

"Did a good job, didn't they?" Sheriff Merz asked.

I could feel a vein in my temple begin to throb with anger. "Who did it?"

The sheriff shrugged. "They were gone by the time anybody found her. Must have come in from the parking lot, beat her up and run out again. They beat up on her too hard, son. She's dead."

I got down beside her. I don't know why I did it. The sheriff was looking at me. He wanted to say something, but didn't. I lifted Gloria Townsend's hand and put a finger on the wrist. At first I wasn't sure, because my hand was trembling.

Then I felt it. A faint but rapid flutter of pulse.

I stood up. "This girl isn't dead, you damned fool! Send for a doctor."

"She's dead, son. Felt for the heartbeat myself."

"Damn you, get a doctor!"

"Don't bust a gut, son. Coroner's coming. He's a doctor."

Just then Gloria Townsend groaned. The sheriff looked at me, then turned and casually spat into the sink. "Well, what do you know about that?" he said.

I couldn't help wondering what would have happened if I hadn't come.

chapter four

THE COUNTY CORONER arrived a few minutes later, a sharp, waspish little man named Dr. Samuel Bowers. Usually politicians stick together, and coroner is just as much a political job as sheriff. But apparently Bowers was a doctor first and a politician second. He took one look at Gloria Townsend and turned the air blue.

"You said over the phone you had a corpse!" he yelled at Sheriff Merz. "I'd have been here twenty minutes ago if I'd known the woman was alive. Get those ambulance attendants in here with a stretcher. Fast!"

The sheriff jumped as though someone had given him a hotfoot. He didn't have to take orders from the coroner, but he decided to anyway. Unlocking the door to the parking lot, he trotted off like an obedient messenger boy. I didn't blame him. The waspish little doctor was in such a towering rage, I think I'd have jumped to run an errand too, if he had snapped an order at me.

An ambulance had showed up because the county didn't own a morgue wagon. When a corpse had to be delivered to the county morgue, they sent an ambulance from Ross Memorial Hospital, the county hospital. This one had come expecting a leisurely trip back to the morgue. Instead it headed for Ross Memorial Hospital with its siren wide open.

Dr. Bowers rode off in the ambulance with Gloria, and Sheriff Merz returned to his old laconic self as soon as the coroner was gone.

"Well, son, guess that winds this up here," he said to me.

"Winds them up?" I said. "You haven't even started your investigation yet."

He shrugged. "Can't do much until the gal gets conscious so I can talk to her."

"You could check this rest room for fingerprints. With all this tile and porcelain, practically anywhere you touch would leave a print."

He snorted. "Must be a couple of dozen people a day

come in here. Couldn't sort out all the prints in a million years."

I pointed to the broken-heeled shoe in the sink. "Somebody held that in his hand when he beat the girl. It's black patent leather, a perfect surface for prints."

He glowered at me. "Listen, son, I know how to run an investigation. Don't really need advice from a city boy. Suppose you scoot along home and let me run the police business in my own territory."

There wasn't anything I could do about it. I didn't have any more authority in the county than I'd have had if the beating had taken place in Moscow. I went out the door into the parking lot without even saying good-bye. I left the door open behind me, and a few yards away I glanced back over my shoulder.

Sheriff Merz had picked up the shoe and was examining it thoughtfully, turning it over and over in his big hands and effectively smearing any possible prints.

On the way back to town I stopped for some lunch. It was just one thirty when I drove the Merc back into the City Hall garage. Upstairs I stalked into Sunshine Sever's office and dumped the whole story in his lap.

"This guy Merz is an incompetent nincompoop," I said. "That girl would have died if it had been left to him. He has no intention whatever of even going through the motions of an investigation."

"Now don't get steamed up," Sunshine advised. "It's his problem, not ours. We've got enough crime in our own territory to worry about."

"But this has bearing on a city problem, Sunshine. I can't get to first base on this call-girl investigation if I have to stop at the city limits. It's headquartered in the county, but it operates here in town. You want me just to drop the whole thing?"

"No, no, Mike. I want this call-girl racket cracked. But you tromp on too many people's toes. First you risk getting the Morals Division down on us, now you want to start a war with the sheriff's department. This office can't function without the cooperation of other agencies, Mike. You've got to learn to get along with them. I don't mean to hamstring your investigation, but you've got to stay within our own jurisdiction."

"Nuts," I said. "Then I might as well fold up." I went

out, slamming his door to let him know how I felt, and
went into my own office.

I phoned the county hospital to ask about Gloria Townsend and got the routine mumbo-jumbo that the patient
was "as well as can be expected at this point." When I
asked if that meant she was critical, the nurse I was talking
to said her condition wasn't yet listed because diagnosis
wasn't complete.

In other words, they didn't yet know how bad off she
was.

Then I phoned the Morals Division and got hold of
Lieutenant Stan Spooner. I try to keep on friendly terms
with the whole police department, and the head of the
Morals Division was no exception. Stan Spooner was a quiet,
reserved man, however, a pleasant enough guy but one hard
to know well. While we were on a first-name basis and I'd
always gotten excellent co-operation from him, there was
a touch of formality in him which discouraged close friend-
ship.

"Oh, hello, Mike," he said in his pleasant but reserved
way. "What can I do for you?"

"My interview with Harry Allerup was interrupted by
some other business that came up unexpectedly this morning,
Stan," I said. "Could I have him over again?"

The lieutenant's voice sounded regretful. "Gee, Mike, I
wish I'd known you weren't through with him. He went
on a three-day leave starting at noon today, and there's
no way to reach him. He's spending it up at his river cottage, where there's no phone."

"Oh," I said. "When's he due back?"

"What's today? Thursday? He comes back on the day
trick Monday morning. Want to give me a ring then?"

"All right," I said, and rang off.

There didn't seem to be anything more I could do at
the moment on the call-girl investigation, and since it was
only supposed to be an extra activity, for the rest of the
day I lost myself in routine work. As my trip to the Lagoon
had taken the whole morning, it was after ten P.M. before
I caught up enough to call it a day.

The first thing next morning I called Ross Memorial
Hospital again to check on Gloria Townsend. By now she'd
been under observation long enough to rate a listing. She
was listed as critical. The nurse I talked to was a little

reluctant to give out any more information than that until I told her who I was. Apparently the county hospital wasn't as jurisdiction-conscious as the Sheriff's Department, because she opened up then.

Gloria Townsend was still unconscious from what was probably a brain concussion, but possibly was a fractured skull. X-rays showed no other broken bones, but there were possible internal injuries. It would be at least another twenty-four hours before anything more definite would be known.

I asked the nurse's name so that I could inquire for her again the next time I called. She said it was Miss Henning and that she was charge nurse in ward 2-B, where Gloria Townsend was.

After I hung up, I thought, for a few moments, then had an idea. Telling Miss Rains I'd be back in a few minutes, I took the elevator down and walked the half block up City Hall Street to Stacy's Bar.

Stacy's is just an ordinary neighborhood tavern with nothing to set it apart from a thousand like it except the proprietor. George Stacy, a tall, thin man with a remarkable resemblance to Basil Rathbone, has let the resemblance affect his personality. He once saw Rathbone play Sherlock Holmes, and ever since he's been a frustrated detective. He always has the murder cases he reads about in the newspapers solved before the police do, and the fact that his batting average to date is zero doesn't seem to discourage his sublime faith in his deductive ability. He loves conspiracy, and all you have to do to get his undivided attention is drop your voice and glance around furtively when you speak to him.

I often use the device to get service when the place is jammed. Today, at nine-thirty in the morning, it was empty except for me, but I used it anyway.

Shaking my head at Stacy's question as to what I wanted to drink, I asked in a low voice, "The address c/o Smith, R.F.D. Two mean anything to you, George?"

He gave a conspiratorial glance around. "The place out on Rivershore Drive?"

"That's it. Got any contacts there?"

He had to struggle between his love of conspiracy and his wariness at admitting even a remote connection with the call-girl racket to a member of the D.A.'s staff. His love of conspiracy won out.

"Sometimes I steer a customer out there if he asks where to find a woman," he admitted. "Just as a service, understand. I don't get no kickback. Tupper Smith accepts my name as an introduction. Why?"

"Well," I said, attempting to look self-conscious. "I'm in a kind of funny position, George. I have to be careful if I want to cut loose a little. It would look like the devil if it ever got out that a member of the D.A.'s staff patronized a place like that."

"Oh," he said with a look of enlightenment. "Want me to fix you up for a weekend?"

"Not under my own name," I said. "Think you could arrange for one of the girls to meet me at a hotel? Sort of make out that I'm a visiting fireman?"

"Sure," he said. "Nothing to it." He paused a moment. "Those girls are top-quality stuff though, Mike. A weekend will rock you two hundred bucks."

"I know it," I told him. "I'll register at the Graham under the name Michael Ford. See if you can fix it up for nine P.M. tonight."

"You're the doctor," Stacy said. "Stick around and I'll call in right now."

chapter five

I CHECKED INTO the Graham Hotel shortly after five, had dinner in the hotel dining room, then showered and dressed for my professional date. When I was all ready, I discovered I had a full two hours to wait. I spent it watching TV in the hotel room.

Promptly at nine the room phone rang. When I lifted it, a clear feminine voice said, "Mr. Ford?"

"Speaking."

"My name is Penny Coynes, Mr. Ford. I'm phoning from the lobby. Do you want me to come up, or would you rather meet me in the bar?"

"I'll meet you in the bar," I decided. "How do I recognize you?"

"I'm blonde, I'm wearing an upsweep and I have on a green-and-white dress. How will I know you?"

"I'll carry a rose in my teeth," I said. "See you in two minutes."

The hotel bar was crowded, but I picked her out at once. She was a slim, delicate-featured blonde in a light green-and-white summer print. She was somewhere in her mid-twenties, but the stiff, school-girl way she perched on her bar stool, as though she wasn't used to sitting at bars, made her seem even younger. Her upswept hair-do gave her the fresh, innocent look of a sub-deb. In her lap she held one of those huge, cone-shaped bags which close by a draw-string, the kind women carry when they are carting around too much stuff for a purse to hold but not enough to require a suitcase. It was of the same material and design as her dress.

Stopping behind her, I said, "Hello, Penny."

She turned slowly, almost with reluctance, as though bracing herself for a plunge. I suppose when a girl sells herself sight unseen, she goes through a little mental turmoil wondering what she's sold herself to.

After looking me over, her expression turned relieved. She smiled approvingly, exposing small, perfect teeth.

"I don't see the rose," she said.

"The sight of you so overwhelmed me, I swallowed it," I said. "Shall we take a booth?"

Obediently she slipped from her stool, and I led her to a booth in a corner of the room. I ordered drinks, then we just sat there smilingly examining each other until the waiter brought them and went away again.

"I'm a little surprised," I said finally. "I didn't expect such young innocence. Sure you're old enough to be in the business you are?"

She flushed. A little defensively she said, "Did you expect something hard-boiled? You can get that for a lot less than two hundred dollars."

"Oh, yes," I said. "I almost forgot that part." Reaching in my pocket, I pulled out the four fifties I had already folded together and casually dropped my hand on the table, my palm covering all but a corner of the folded bills. "Just pretend to squeeze my hand and nobody will see the transfer."

She flushed even deeper. "I didn't mean it like that. I wasn't dunning you."

She was surprising me more by the minute. I said, "Sorry I injected such a harsh commercial note, but isn't it the custom to pay in advance?"

She looked as though she was going to cry.

I changed my tone. "I really am sorry," I said sincerely. "I'm not trying to make you feel like a tramp. But there is a business deal that has to be settled sometime. I'd just as soon get it over with, so we can start from scratch. Unless you want to make it a free weekend and pay your employer's cut out of your own pocket."

Her eyes touched mine, then dropped to the table. "You know I can't do that," she said in a low voice. "It's just that I hate this part. I—I guess I'm not very good at this business yet."

Tired of holding my hand in the center of the table, I lifted one of hers with my free hand, pressed the bills into her palm and held her hand in both of mine for a moment. Any nearby observers would probably have thought I was proposing. Not necessarily proposing marriage, but proposing something.

When I released her hand, she dropped it into her lap. I heard the slithering noise the drawstrings of her bag made as she pulled open its mouth and then drew it shut again. Her eyes avoided mine.

"What did you mean by 'yet'?" I asked. "How long have you been in the business?"

"You're only my third customer. My fourth, really, except I wouldn't take one. Mr. Smith was awfully mad. That's my boss, Mr. Smith. He said if I ever turned down another customer when I went out on a call, he'd—well, he said not to do it. I was so glad when I saw you. I almost get sick wondering what a man will be like."

"I suppose it is like playing grab-bag," I said. "What was the matter with the customer you turned down?"

"He was—well, greasy-looking. I just couldn't go with him."

"Why do you stay in the business if you're so squeamish?"

"How else could I earn two hundred dollars every week-end? A hundred and fifty, rather, after Mr. Smith's fee."

"Couldn't you live on less?" I asked dryly.

Her chin went up and she looked at me levelly. "I do

live on less. Weekdays you'll find me modeling dresses at Stoyle's Department Store. I only do this weekends. And every cent I make from it goes to my sister in California."

I looked at her blankly. "You mean you do this solely to support a sister?"

"Not support," she said. "Anita broke her back in an auto accident three years ago. She's completely paralyzed, and she's been in and out of hospitals ever since, having one operation after another by high-priced specialists. Her hospitalization insurance ran out long ago. She has four children, and her husband has mortgaged everything he owns to pay bills. She needs one final operation to make her walk again, but they've reached the absolute end of their rope. If I don't send the money, she won't have it."

I never met a prostitute who didn't have some heart-rending excuse for being in the business. One of the standard ones is needing money for an operation, usually on a poor old mother.

Penny Coynes' story had the ring of truth, though. You could question her judgment in selling her body to aid a sister, for it was hardly the sort of sacrifice the average woman would even consider, regardless of the urgency of the situation. But I didn't question her sincerity.

I'm not a sucker for sob stories. As an assistant D.A. I've heard too many. I even once had an axe murderer try to work me into sympathetic understanding of why he was driven to his crime. I've also heard enough to spot the phony ones.

I believed Penny Coynes' story.

She gave a little forced laugh. "That's a fine way to give you your money's worth. Telling you my troubles. You've paid for a good time, and you're going to get it. How are we going to spend the weekend?"

I looked at her and raised an eyebrow and she blushed. "Well, that I know," she said. "Is that all you want to do? You want to take me up to your room now?"

She was making an heroic attempt to give me my money's worth, all right. I'd paid the fee, so she was mine for the weekend, to do with as I pleased. But it took effort for her to be matter-of-fact about it. She wasn't exactly scared. By her own admission I was at least her third customer, so she couldn't have been. But she was at least self-conscious. I suppose some women could never get used to selling themselves, even after the thousandth time.

I said, "We have the whole weekend. How about another drink now?"

We had three, and she was becoming a little tipsy by the time the third was down. It didn't detract from her, though. It only made her cuter. She began to sparkle like a diamond bracelet.

Then, just as we were getting really chummy, a shadow loomed over us and a reserved voice said, "Evening, Mike. I didn't know the Graham was one of your hangouts."

We both looked up, and my heart sank when I recognized the round, pink-and-white face of Lieutenant Stan Spooner. He was looking curiously at Penny Coynes.

There wasn't anything I could do except introduce him. I mumbled, "Stan Spooner," deliberately leaving out his title, then nodded toward Penny and said, "Miss Coynes, Stan."

He said he was glad to meet her, in his quietly pleasant way, and refused my reluctant offer to buy him a drink with the remark that he didn't want to intrude. I thought he was going to move on without giving me away, when he spoiled everything.

He said to Penny, "Hope you and Mr. Macauley have a pleasant evening, Miss Coynes."

That blew it. When the lieutenant, innocent of the bomb he had dropped, moved on toward the bar, Penny examined me from narrowed eyes.

"So it's Mike Macauley instead of Mike Ford, is it, Mr. Assistant District Attorney. You're the man Gloria Townsend was dealing with. What is this? Another attempt to break up our business?"

chapter six

SHE STARTED TO OPEN her bag and reach into it for the four fifties I had given her, but I held up a hand and she paused long enough to stare at me.

"Don't go off half-cocked," I said rapidly. "The fake name was just to keep me out of trouble. Think your friend Smith would have sent you along if I'd given my real name?"

She examined my face for a long time, finally said, "Are you trying to tell me you really just wanted to let your hair down? This isn't some kind of an undercover investigation?"

I said, "I have no intention of getting you up to my room, having you undress and then arresting you, like Harry Allerup did to Gloria Townsend. I'll leave that kind of work to the Morals Division cops. What difference does it make who I am? You have your fee, and you said I don't revolt you. Wouldn't you rather earn it from me than take a chance on your next customer being a greasy fat man?"

She continued to look at me doubtfully. "You're in charge of the call-girl investigation. Everybody knows that."

"Sure. Eventually I hope to crack it. But it wouldn't crack it to toss you in jail. I promise I won't get you in trouble."

She hesitated, undecided whether to return my fee and leave, or stick it out. I think my suggestion that her next customer might be less pleasant finally decided her.

"I'm probably crazy," she said. "I believe you are making some kind of undercover investigation. But I think I trust you too. I don't think you'd arrest me after promising you wouldn't."

I grinned at her. "Now that we're friends again, want another drink?"

She shook her head. "Not here, now that I know who you are. You aren't the only one who could be recognized by a friend. And I wouldn't want it to get back to Mr. Smith that I was hobnobbing with an assistant D.A. Let's get out of sight."

By out of sight, she obviously meant my room. I took her up to it and ordered a couple of highballs from room service.

While waiting for our order, Penny opened her large bag, drew out a filmy lace nightgown and neatly folded it under one of the pillows of the double bed. After she carried a toothbrush into the bathroom, her moving-in seemed to be complete.

When she came from the bathroom, she cocked her head to one side and examined me curiously.

"What's the matter?" I asked.

"You're an odd one, Mike Macauley. You haven't even kissed me hello yet."

Stepping toward her, I took her shoulders and looked down into her face. "Hello, Penny Coynes."

She raised her lips as innocently as a teen-ager offering a good-night kiss to her date after the high-school prom. But when they touched mine, they became the lips of a woman. One instant they were cool and gentle, the next hot and demanding. Her arms went about my neck and her body strained against mine. She began to tremble as my hands drifted over her body.

A knock came at the door.

We broke reluctantly, her hands lightly sliding across each side of my face in a final caress as she moved away. Her eye pupils were enormously dilated and her soft lips slightly parted. It was no simulated professional act. There was genuine desire in her face.

Wiping lipstick from my mouth with a handkerchief, I opened the door to admit the room-service waiter. He carried in his tray, set the two highballs on the dresser and handed me the tab. I overtipped him and got him out again.

When the door closed, Penny and I looked at each other. There was a waiting expression on her face. There may have been one on mine too, but I suppressed it. I had brought her up here to learn something about the call-girl racket, and business came before pleasure.

"Better not let the ice melt," I said, lifting one of the drinks and handing it to her.

She looked a little disappointed, but she accepted the drink. I raised mine, said, "Bumps," and we both sipped.

"You mentioned Gloria Townsend before," I said. "Know her well?"

Her expression became a little wary. "Pretty well. She was one of the girls."

"Was? She isn't dead."

She studied the ice in her highball. "No. But close to it. I don't imagine she'll come back to work if she recovers."

"She'd be a fool if she did," I said. "You know who beat her up, don't you?"

She gave me a frightened look. "Do you?"

"Not by name. But it was someone in the organization you work for. To keep her from talking to me."

Her expression relaxed at the news that I didn't know the actual assailant. "Tupper Smith has a different theory."

"The farmer whose place you girls use for a headquarters?

He would have, since it was probably on his order that Gloria was beaten. What's his story?"

"He thinks Gloria's brother beat her because he found out she was a call girl. Sid Trask."

"She has a brother named Trask?"

Penny nodded. "That's her real name too. Gladys Trask. Sid's the yard manager at Sullivan's Lumber Company. He's a huge man and has a violent temper. He'd be quite capable of beating her if he found out what she was doing."

I snorted. "The girl was going to give me some inside dope on the racket. The beating stopped her. It would be pretty coincidental if an outraged brother came along just in time to get Tupper Smith and his cohorts off the hook."

Penny drained her glass, set it down on the dresser and said, "You didn't really make this date to let your hair down, did you? You just want to pump me. Would you like to see me beaten like Gloria?"

The minute she made the remark, she wished she hadn't. She looked at me in consternation.

"So you know the real reason she was beaten," I said softly. "Didn't it scare you a little to see what happens to girls who want to quit? Won't you want to quit some day, Penny?"

The question jolted her. You could tell by her suddenly pinched and withdrawn expression that it was one she had skirted because she was afraid to face it.

"Let's change the subject, Mike. If you just want to pump me, I'll give you your money back and go home."

I set down my glass. "Come here," I ordered.

She came to me obediently, standing before me like a little girl, with averted eyes. I took her shoulders and drew her into my arms. Her lips raised, but it wasn't like before. She was unresisting, but without passion.

After a moment I raised my head and looked down into her upturned face. She waited, her eyes closed and her expression remote.

"It's no good, is it, Penny?" I asked quietly.

Her eyes opened. "Why, Mike?"

"Because before you wanted me. Now you're just offering what's paid for. And I think I like you too much to buy you."

She gazed at me steadily, her lips barely parted. "Do you,

Mike? You mean you'd only want me if it wasn't a business arrangement?"

"That's about the size of it, Penny."

"But you would want me then?"

"Who wouldn't?" I said a little bitterly. "You're a lovely girl."

Disengaging herself from my arms, she picked up her conical bag and drew out the two hundred dollars. Separating one of the fifties, she returned it to the bag and laid the other three on the dresser.

"Tupper Smith's cut for the referral is fifty," she said. "Now there's no profit in it for me."

I shook my head wonderingly. "For a call girl you're the poorest businesswoman I ever heard of. Stop trying to give me my money back every few minutes. You've kept your part of the bargain. It's my loss if I don't want to take advantage of it."

She watched me quietly, looking a little lost, as I picked up the bills and dropped them back in the bag.

I said, "What's your real name, Penny?"

"It's Coynes. The Penny is faked, but the last name is right. Peggy Coynes."

"Then next time I'll take you out as Peggy Coynes the dress model, instead of as Penny Coynes the call girl. I think we'd both like it better."

She went over to the bed, drew the filmy nightgown from beneath the pillow, went to the bathroom and returned with her toothbrush. She stowed both away in her bag without looking at me. She started for the door, stopped with her hand on the knob and suddenly turned and ran to me.

"Mike," she said, "be careful. Be awfully careful."

She gave me a quick kiss, ran back to the door and was gone.

chapter seven

THE NEXT MORNING, Saturday, I phoned Ross Memorial Hospital again and talked to Miss Henning. She said it had now been determined that Gloria Townsend had only a concussion instead of a skull fracture, and her condition was listed as fair. She had regained consciousness, she had no serious internal injuries, but she wouldn't be allowed visitors for several days yet. Barring complications, it was expected she would be completely recovered in about a week.

The District Attorney's office closes at noon on Saturdays, so I decided to use the afternoon for a visit to Sheriff Merz's office. I took my own car instead of an official car for the twenty-mile drive to the county seat.

The village of Rawley is an old-fashioned place built around a village square. The ancient courthouse is in the center of the square, and the sheriff's office is on the first floor of the courthouse.

None of the county agencies aside from the sheriff's office was open on Saturday afternoons. I walked along the deserted corridor until I spotted the sign I was looking for, opened a frosted-glass door and found myself in a large waiting room. A complaint desk ran the width of the room to my right, and beyond it were the bars of three detention cells, all vacant and with their doors standing open. To my left were two huge windows. Centered between them was the panel, switches, dials and microphone of a modern sending-and-receiving short-wave set. Directly across from me was a door labeled "Private."

The western-style deputy I had clashed with at the Lagoon sat behind the complaint desk, looking just as much like a hero of the old west except that he wasn't wearing his Stetson.

He frowned when he looked up and recognized me, and I said, "Hi there, podner. Sheriff Merz around?"

"What you want with him?"

"Let's not go through that again," I said wearily. "Is he in, or isn't he?"

"Over there," he said shortly, pointing to the door marked "Private."

Probably the sheriff expected visitors to knock, but I just opened the door and walked in. Sheriff Merz was seated behind an oversized desk reading reports, his faded denim work shirt open halfway down his chest to expose the mat of graying hair which covered his body. He scowled at me, then leaned back in his chair with his arms resting along the wooden arm rests, an expression of weary patience on his face. He didn't say anything.

"Afternoon, Sheriff," I said, taking a seat in the wooden chair in front of his desk. "Just dropped by to see how the Gloria Townsend investigation is coming."

He stared at me for a time, fiddling with the tuft of hair growing from one of his ears. Presently he said, "Didn't know things that happen in the county were city business, son."

"When they have bearing on things happening in the city they are, Sheriff. You've heard of the call-girl racket operating in the city, I suppose."

"Heard there was one. Never paid much attention. I got my own troubles."

"Then maybe you've heard that while it operates in the city, it operates *out of* the county. The headquarters is a farm out on Rivershore Drive owned by a man named Tupper Smith."

The sheriff snorted. "Where'd you get that idea, son? There's no cat houses operating in my territory."

"I didn't say it was a cat house. It's just the clerical center for the call-girl racket, so far as I know. Tupper Smith is too smart to let his girls keep dates anywhere except inside the city limits. He keeps himself clean insofar as the county is concerned. The only way to crack his setup is for the city and the county to co-operate."

Merz scratched the scanty strip of hair behind his ears. "Don't see how I can help you, son. If he isn't working his racket in this county, I can't touch him."

"And we can't touch him because he works from beyond the city limits," I said angrily. "Oh, sure, the Morals Division can pull in one of his girls now and then, if they go to the trouble of setting up a date and catching her in the act of accepting money. Except there's only six men on the Morals Squad, and the girls probably have been given descriptions of all of them. And even when one is nailed, all she gets is a suspended sentence. Unless you and I co-operate, we can't touch Smith himself."

Sheriff Merz said, "Well, if I ever hear of a call girl meeting a date in my territory, I'll raid this feller's place and see what I find. About all I can do for you."

"In other words, nothing, eh? What have you done about Gloria Townsend?"

Sheriff Merz tugged at the hair sticking from his other ear.

"I told you that was strictly a county case, son. No business of the city."

"She's one of Tupper Smith's call girls," I said. "She wanted out of the racket and was going to spill everything she knew to me. That's why I was meeting her at the Lagoon. She was beaten to stop her from talking."

He raised hairy eyebrows. "Sounds kind of far-fetched to me, son. But I'll ask her about it when she's well enough to talk."

"Find any fingerprints on that shoe?" I asked sarcastically.

He shook his head. "Not a print."

"Not even your own?" I inquired. "Last I saw, you were smearing your hands all over it."

He frowned at me.

I said, "Since it's pretty obvious I'm not going to get co-operation from you anyway, I might as well stop being polite and get a couple of things off my chest. Your handling of this case smells, Sheriff. Either you're incompetent, or you deliberately obstructed evidence by handling that shoe. I'm inclined to think the latter. A racket like this call-girl thing can't exist without the connivance of local authorities. I think you're getting a rake-off from Tupper Smith, and I think you know exactly why that girl was beaten. You may even know who did it. You even went so far in covering up, you were willing to let the girl die. I think you knew damned well she wasn't dead, and deliberately held off calling a doctor."

His face had been getting redder and redder as I spoke. By the time I finished, he was on the verge of apoplexy.

Slamming back his chair, he came erect and yelled, "Get out of here, you meddling son-of-a-bitch! Get out and stay out!"

I came erect too. "Why don't you throw me out, Sheriff? I think I'd enjoy that more."

He started to lumber around his desk, but stopped when he saw the expression on my face.

"Gordy!" he yelled.

There was movement in the outer room, then the western-type deputy opened the door. He looked inquiringly at the sheriff.

Sheriff Merz was momentarily unable to speak. His rage had paralyzed his vocal cords. His mouth made motions like a fish kissing the side of a bowl, but no sound came out.

Finally he managed to squeak, "Throw this son-of-a-bitch in the street, Gordy."

Gordy looked me up and down warily. He was a tall, rangily-built guy with enough muscle on him to take care of himself, but he didn't have the spirit to go with the muscle. He didn't seem to like the look on my face any better than the sheriff had.

"Now let's not have any trouble around here," he said. "The sheriff says to get out of here, mister. You better go along."

I walked toward where he stood in the doorway. He eyed my approach uncertainly, but stood his ground. Two feet from him I stuck my face in his and said, "Boo!"

He jumped about a foot in the air, sidestepped and left the doorway clear. I went on through without looking back at either of them.

chapter eight

THE FIRST THING Monday morning I phoned headquarters and asked for the Morals Division. Lieutenant Spooner wasn't in, and neither was Harry Allerup. I left word asking for the first one who showed to call me back.

A few minutes later Sunshine Sever called me onto the carpet in his office. He wasn't beaming any ray of sunshine today. His scowl was as black as a hurricane warning.

He waved a piece of paper at me and said, "Mike, I've got a formal complaint here from Sheriff Merz's office. What in the devil did you say to the man?"

"Just called him the crook he is."

The district attorney rose from his desk and prowled up and down the room with his hands clasped behind his back in overweight imitation of Felix the Cat. "Look, Mike," he said in the patient tone of a grade-school teacher explaining a simple problem to the class dunce, "I've told you I like to keep friendly relations with other agencies. You can't walk into a neighboring law-enforcement officer's personal sanctum and throw around wild accusations."

"They weren't wild," I said. "It's obvious he's collecting a payoff from Tupper Smith."

"Can you prove it?" he snapped at me.

Reluctantly I shook my head. "He has to be, Sunshine. Smith couldn't operate without his protection."

Sunshine shook his head too, sadly and reproachfully. "You're a law graduate, Mike. You know better than to make an accusation without evidence. Merz could sue you for defamation of character."

"He hasn't any character," I said. "Besides, there weren't any witnesses."

He looked a little relieved. "At least that's something. I hate to do this, Mike, but you won't take my suggestions, so I'm making it an order. Stay within the city limits."

I hiked a couple of eyebrows. "During duty hours, you mean."

"I mean any time."

I shook my head regretfully. "This isn't Russia, and you're no commissar, comrade. I take your orders up to five P.M. After that I'm a private citizen. If you think I'm asking your permission to dine at some county roadhouse, or take a drive along the river, guess again."

"You know that isn't what I mean," he said impatiently. "Just stay out of the county as a representative of this office. I mean it, Mike. You clash with Merz again, and I won't back you up an inch."

"How about this time?" I asked. "Going to write him a nice long apology?"

He said shortly, "I'm going to acknowledge receipt of his complaint. Period. No comment one way or the other."

I grinned at him. Sunshine liked to keep inter-agency peace, but he didn't like to kowtow. Despite his threat, I knew that if it came to a showdown, the D.A. would stand behind me like a rock.

"I probably won't see Merz again anyway," I told him. "There isn't much point in butting my head against a wall."

By noon, when I still hadn't heard from either Lieutenant Spooner or Harry Allerup, I called the Morals Division again. I got hold of Spooner.

"You were going to send Allerup over for a talk this morning," I reminded him.

"Jeepers, Mike," he said with a mixture of embarrassment and regret. "I guess I goofed everything up. I was out all morning, and while I was gone the chief of detectives glooped him off for a special assignment. He's on his way to Chicago to pick up a prisoner."

"Nuts," I said heartily.

"I'm really sorry," Spooner said. "It never occurred to me something like that would happen, so I didn't leave word with anybody that you wanted to see Allerup. I thought I'd just tell him myself."

"Well, it can't be helped," I told him. "When's he due back?"

"Not till Wednesday night. I'll have him over to your office Thursday morning for sure."

"Okay, Stan," I said. "Thanks."

Later that day I phoned the county hospital and learned that Gloria Townsend was now allowed visitors. I decided to hit Ross Memorial Hospital during the seven-to-eight visiting hour that evening. I needled Sunshine a little by telling him I was making the call not as an assistant D.A., but as a friend of the family.

He only grunted.

At Ross Memorial Hospital I made my way to ward 2-B and asked a passing nurse where I could find Miss Henning, the nurse who had been keeping me posted on Gloria's condition. She said Miss Henning worked the day trick, so I asked for Gloria's room number. She was in two thirty-six.

Two thirty-six was a single room and Gloria was sitting up in bed. There were still bruises on her face, but the swelling had died and, except for a couple of discolored spots, she looked as beautiful as ever. Her long tawny hair was carefully brushed, she wore a touch of makeup and she had on a frilly bed jacket.

She had two other visitors, a man and a woman. The woman, a lushly-built redhead with catlike green eyes and a full, sensuous mouth, looked me over calculatingly when I entered the room, judging my build, my clothes and my bank balance. Some women can't help looking at every man they see like that.

The man was enormous. He must have gone six feet six and over two hundred and fifty pounds. He had thick, unimaginative features, somewhat battered shoulders which made him look as though he wore football pads and no fat on him. Both the man and the woman were dressed expensively.

Gloria looked at me without much enthusiasm and said, "Oh, hello, Mr. Macauley."

She introduced the man as her brother, Sid Trask, and the woman as Alice Dill. My first assumption, probably because of the calculating look she had given me, was that the red-head was a fellow call girl of Gloria's, but then I got the impression that she was Sid Trask's girl friend.

Alice Dill said, "Mike Macauley? Seems to me I've seen that name in the papers. Aren't you with the District Attorney's office?"

"I'm an assistant D.A.," I admitted.

Up to then the enormous Sid Trask had accepted me on probation, reserving judgment until he found out who I was and what I wanted. Now he glowered at me.

I said to Gloria, "How you feeling, Gloria?"

Before she could tell me, Sid Trask growled in the husky voice of a man who has been hit once too often in the Adam's apple, "What's this Gloria stuff, mister? Why's she registered as Gloria Townsend, when her name's Gladys Trask? And what business has the District Attorney's office got with her?"

I decided to ignore the first question and answer the second. "What makes you think it has any? Maybe I just stopped in as a friend."

This didn't mollify him much. "A friend who don't know her right name? You haven't answered the first question, mister."

I shrugged. "You'll have to ask your sister. The identification on her said Gloria Townsend."

"I have asked her." He turned to the girl in the bed. "For cripes sake, Sis, what's this all about? Stop giving me the runaround."

"Please, Sid, not now. You're giving me a headache." She pressed the back of one hand to her brow. "It's just a name I was using to try for an acting job. I told you."

"Acting job hell," he said huskily. "You don't change your driver's license and identification card and stuff when you take a stage name. You been up to something, and I want to know what."

"Later, Sid. After I feel better."

The red-haired Alice Dill said, "Leave her alone now, Sid. She's been through enough."

I managed to insert a question to Gloria as to whether or not she recognized whoever had beaten her.

She shook her head wearily. "I didn't even see them. I was standing at the sink when they came through the door from the parking lot. I started to glance up, and something hit me alongside the neck. I think it was a judo chop."

"You didn't see anything at all?" I asked. "You don't even know how many there were?"

"At least two," she said. "A man and a woman. I got a bare glimpse of their feet as I went down. I think it must have been the woman who came in first and hit me in the neck. Or maybe I just imagined that because it was the ladies' room, and I assumed whoever was coming in the door was female."

Sid Trask said, "She's already told all this to Sheriff Merz. Leave her alone."

I looked at him. "Don't you care who beat your sister?"

He was seated in a chair on the opposite side of the bed, and Alice Dill was seated in the window sill alongside of him. He started to get out of his chair, but the redhead pushed him back again.

I said to Gloria, "We won't talk about it now, in front of your company, but are you still willing to tell me what you were going to?"

"I don't know. I'll have to think about it." Her eyes warned me to drop the subject.

"Think about what?" Trask asked. "What were you going to tell this guy, Sis?"

Gloria simply ignored him.

I said, "Has it occurred to you, Gloria—Gladys—that when you get out of here, the same people may be waiting to work you over again?"

Gloria looked frightened and Sid Trask made a growling noise deep in his throat.

"Well, has it?" I insisted.

She said in a low voice, "Yes."

"For your own safety I have a suggestion," I said. "Suppose I pick you up personally when you're ready to leave the hospital, and hide you in some hotel in town? I'll arrange a police watch to protect you."

"Listen, Buster," Sid Trask said. "When she's ready to leave the hospital, I'll pick her up and take care of her. I wouldn't be surprised if it was the cops themselves who beat her up.

Or maybe even you. What's this stuff about Gladys telling you something? You people been giving her a third-degree?"

Ignoring him, I continued to look at Gloria.

"I—I don't know what to do, Mr. Macauley. I'll have to think about it. I'll be here several days yet."

Her brother demanded, "What's this information you want, Macauley?"

Alice Dill said thoughtfully, "You know what Mr. Macauley's current project is, Sid? It was in the papers."

"What?" he asked.

"The call-girl racket."

Sid Trask stared at her for a moment, then he stared at me for a while, then he surged to his feet. This time the redhead's push didn't sit him down again.

"Why, you bastard," he said to me. "You say my sister's a call girl and I'll knock your silly head off."

"I didn't say it," I said reasonably. "Your girl friend did. Why don't you knock her head off?"

He started around the bed and Gloria said sharply, "Sid!"

He stopped long enough to look at her.

Gloria said, "You start a rumpus in here and I'll ring for the nurse and have you barred from future visiting. Now sit down."

He stared at her for a time, then went back to his seat. He said to me, "I'll look you up outside the hospital, Buster. Expect me."

There wasn't much point in staying longer, because I obviously wasn't going to accomplish anything with the brother there. I told Gloria I'd be back another time and left.

chapter nine

DURING THE DRIVE BACK to town, I brooded myself into a bad mood. It seemed as though everywhere I turned in this investigation I ran into a wall of opposition, even from people who logically should want to co-operate.

Sheriff Merz I could understand, because I was convinced he was tied in with the call-girl racket at least to the extent of officially ignoring it in return for a payoff. But I didn't seem to be able to get any better results from people who should have been on my side than I did from the sheriff. Stan Spooner, for instance. The fact that the head of the Morals Division was a co-operative guy didn't alter the fact that he couldn't seem to get me an interview with Harry Allerup, even though Allerup was on his squad and presumably took orders from him. The reasons for Allerup's continued unavailability sounded on the up-and-up, but I wondered if someone higher up than Spooner wasn't pulling strings to keep me from talking to Allerup.

I wasn't even getting much official co-operation from my own chief. Sunshine Sever, of course, just had a politician's fear of stirring up trouble, but whatever his motive, he wasn't being much help.

My meeting with Sid Trask was the last straw. If my sister had taken the beating Gloria Townsend had, I would have fallen all over myself to aid in the investigation. But the big man's hackles had risen the moment he learned I was an assistant D.A. I wondered if there was a possibility that the theory Penny Coynes had mentioned was right. Maybe Sid Trask's anger at the suggestion that his sister was a call girl was just to cover up the fact that he already knew it, and he was the one who had beaten her.

By the time I got back to town I was so disgusted by my entire lack of progress, I stopped at Stacy's Bar and forgot my troubles over a half-dozen highballs.

It was after one A.M. before I finally decided to call it a night, and past one-thirty when I reached my apartment building over on Wren Avenue.

The drinks hadn't left me even slightly tipsy, but they must have dulled my reactions a bit, for I didn't even wonder why the hall and stairway lights weren't working when I flipped the switch and nothing happened. I just gave them a silent bawling out and made my way up the stairs in the dark.

My flat is on the third floor, and he was waiting for me on the landing between second and third. There is a window there, but it's of frosted glass, and not much moonlight seeped through. Enough for my assailant to see by, because his eyes were adjusted to the darkness, but not enough for eyes which had just finished concentrating on the glare twin headlights made in front of a car.

I didn't even know he was standing there until a smashing blow caught me alongside the jaw. It slammed me backward directly toward the landing window. Instinctively I threw myself sidewise so that my back hit the upright part of the window frame instead of the glass, or I would have crashed right through to fall two and a half stories.

That was about all the defense I was able to manage for the next couple of seconds, though. That first blow started bells ringing and so slowed my co-ordination, I only got my fists half raised before a second blow landed on the other side of my face.

This one brought me to my knees. On the verge of blacking out, I made a desperate grab with both arms and encircled a pair of thick legs. By their feel, I was up against a giant.

A tensing of the legs' muscles sent the message to my numbed brain that a judo chop was on its way toward my neck. I tried to pull my head in like a turtle, but that's hard unless you're a turtle. I only managed to hunch my shoulders enough to take the chop alongside the head instead of in the neck. It almost tore an ear off.

Fighting to retain consciousness, I got my feet braced against the wall behind me, straightened my knees and launched both myself and my invisible attacker like a catapult. In the darkness he hit the stairs first, on his back, and I heard the air whoosh out of him. Then we were tumbling end-over-end, with me still gripping his legs, until we crashed to a stop at the second-floor landing.

I landed on top, released his legs and started to swing at where I thought his head might be. I still couldn't see, though, and he could. My fist sank into an upraised palm, and one of his smashed into the center of my forehead.

I arched over backward, bounced off the stair railing and rolled over onto my hands and knees. I could hear him climbing to his feet, but there wasn't a thing I could do about it. I had just enough consciousness left to keep from collapsing on my face, but not enough to come erect.

Then light gleamed into the far end of the hall from a suddenly-opened doorway, casting a dim glow the length of the hall. Unable to raise my head, I stared stupidly at the pair of large feet in front of my face. One came up in a vicious kick meant for my face. I made no attempt to avoid it because I couldn't move. It was just bad marksmanship that made it land on my chest instead.

I rose half erect, carried upward by the force of the kick, fell to hands and knees again, then gave up and sprawled full-length on my face. I drifted off to sleep to the accompaniment of big feet clattering down the stairs in headlong flight.

I was on my back when I woke up. I stared up groggily at the man in pajamas and robe who bent over me. He held an empty water glass in his hand, and the wetness of my face told me what it was that had brought me around.

His voice seemed to come from a great distance. "You all right, Macauley?"

I lay there for a few moments more, gradually clearing the cobwebs from my brain. I recognized the man in the dressing robe as Jim Gordon, one of my downstairs neighbors. Sitting up, I shook my head from side to side.

"You all right?" he repeated.

Looking up at him, I said waspishly, "If I was all right, I wouldn't be flat on my back."

"I mean are you hurt bad?" he said without resentment, examining me with concern.

I felt of my jaw and my tender ear, shook my head a couple of more times and unsteadily made my feet. "I guess I'll live," I said. "You see the guy who jumped me?"

"Just his back. Opening my door scared him off, I guess. He swung a final kick at you and ran like a rabbit. He was a big guy. Must have gone six five or six. Know who he was?"

"I think so. But he jumped me in the dark and I never got a look at him." I noticed the hall light was now on. "What was the matter with the lights?"

"The bulbs were unscrewed. I tightened them up again. Sure you're all right, now?"

"I don't feel like running the hundred-yard dash," I said. "But I think I can make it up the stairs." I started my wavering way upward, hanging onto the railing.

"Want me to help you to your flat?" Gordon asked.

"I'll make it. Thanks for coming to the rescue."

"Sure, Macauley. Wish I'd heard the commotion sooner. Want me to phone the cops for you?"

I shook my head. "I'll handle it, Gordon. Thanks again."

He stood at the bottom of the stairs watching me until I dragged myself around the landing turn.

Inside my flat I poured myself a stiff shot, then made my painful way to the bathroom, stripped and took inventory of my damage. I was going to have a slightly swollen jaw in the morning, but at least it would be symmetrical, because I had gotten belted equally hard on both sides. My ear was a little red, but the cartilage didn't seem to be smashed, so I didn't think it would develop into a cauliflower ear. I ached dully all over and had a few sharper pains in places, but nothing seemed broken.

After a hot shower and a cold nightcap, I didn't feel any worse than anyone would who had been beaten up by a giant and then had tumbled down a flight of stars.

I didn't report the incident to the police. There wasn't much point in it inasmuch as I couldn't positively identify my assailant. I was reasonably certain it had been Sid Trask, however. After his threat to look me up outside the hospital, it would have been too coincidental for anyone else as big as he was to jump me.

I decided I'd look Gloria's brother up again and see how good he was when we started on an even basis.

chapter ten

THE NEXT MORNING I awoke as stiff as a board. My jaws were only slightly swollen, not enough to be noticeable to anyone who didn't know me, and my ear was barely puffed, but I had a lump in the center of my forehead the size of an egg.

A few bending exercises almost killed me, but they took out some of the kinks. A hot shower followed by a cold one completed the therapy, and I felt reasonably healthy by the time I was dressed.

After breakfast at the Greek Mr. Gallo's around the corner from my flat, I decided not to go to the office that morning. I phoned in and told Miss Rains not to expect me till after lunch.

Then I deliberately violated Sunshine Sever's instructions

by going into the county during duty hours. I drove out to Ross Memorial Hospital to see Gloria Townsend.

I picked the morning because visiting hours were only in the afternoon and evening, and I wanted a chance to talk to the girl without her brother or some other visitor being around. The charge nurse, Miss Henning, had been so co-operative over the phone, I felt reasonably sure I could talk my way in even though it wasn't visiting time.

I ran into another blank wall.

Miss Henning turned out to be a pert brunette of about thirty, brisk and efficient-looking in her starched white uniform. She was co-operative enough, but there wasn't much she could do for me under the circumstances.

"I'm sorry, Mr. Macauley," she said regretfully. "But you're listed as an undesirable visitor for Miss Townsend."

I looked at her with my mouth open. "Who the devil issued an order like that?"

"Dr. Forward, the interne on this ward. At the request of Miss Townsend's brother."

"Sid Trask? Doesn't Miss Townsend have anything to say about it?"

"Well, Mr. Trask is the next of kin, and I gather he convinced Dr. Forward that your visit last night unsettled the patient."

"Where's this Dr. Forward?" I inquired.

Lifting a microphone from her desk, she spoke into it and her voice issued quietly from muted speakers situated in the hallways, so that her message was heard simultaneously all over the hospital.

"Dr. Forward wanted at the charge desk in 2-B. Dr. Forward wanted at the charge desk in 2-B."

A few minutes later a white-coated young man who looked more like a professional wrestler than a doctor stepped off the elevator and marched briskly up to the desk. When Miss Henning introduced us, he gave me a polite handshake.

"Have a little accident, Mr. Macauley?" he asked, examining the lump on my forehead with a clinical eye.

"Nothing serious," I told him. "What's this about barring me from visiting Miss Townsend, Doctor?"

He shook his head regretfully. "Sorry, Mr. Macauley. Mr. Trask complained that your visit last night upset the patient. He indicated that you visited her on the excuse of having some kind of police business with her, and badgered her rather badly. I didn't just accept his word for it, of course. I checked with the patient, who denied that you had badgered her, but admitted your visit upset her because you clashed with her brother. It seemed to be a choice between barring you or Mr. Trask, and after all, he's her brother."

"He's not here now," I said. "That's why I came outside of visiting hours. To see her alone."

"Well, if you had genuine police business, I'd let you see her," the interne said. "But I checked with Sheriff Merz after my talk with Mr. Trask. The sheriff says the investigation of Miss Townsend's beating is a county affair, and you have no legal status in it at all. I'm afraid you'd have to bring a court order of some kind before I could lift the ban."

So between them Sheriff Merz and Sid Trask had thrown another obstacle in my way. In co-operation, I wondered, or for individual motives? There wasn't much I could do about it in either event.

"All right, Doctor," I said a little bitterly. "I suppose I should have expected another door slammed in my face. It isn't a new experience. Sorry I troubled you."

"No trouble at all," he said politely.

That effectively blocked my sole lead on the call-girl racket, I thought as I drove back to town. At least until Thursday morning, when I would finally get to talk to Harry Allerup. Providing no one sent him off on another out-of-town mission before I got to him.

The rest of that day and all day Wednesday I simply blanked the call-girl investigation from my mind, concentrating on my regular work. Thursday morning I decided to stop at police headquarters on the way to the office and see if I could catch Allerup before something else came up to make him unavailable.

This time there was no runaround. I found Harry Allerup in the muster room talking to Lieutenant Stan Spooner.

"Good morning, Mike," Spooner said in his courteously formal tone. "I was just telling Allerup to get over to your office. But you may as well talk to him here, now that you're here." He walked off toward his office.

Allerup regarded the still slightly-apparent bruise on my forehead. "Run into a door, Mike?" he asked with the same ease of manner he used to show me before the unsatisfactory session at my office. There was none of the stiffness apparent on that occasion in his tone.

"Fell down a flight of stairs," I said. "You're a kind of hard man to pin down, Harry."

"Yeah. If it isn't leave, I'm guarding prisoners. What did you want to see me about, Mike?"

"The same thing we started to talk about before. Gloria Townsend."

He raised a couple of eyebrows. "Gladys Trask, you mean. What about my future wife?"

I looked at him blankly. "Your what?"

"Future wife, fiancée, bride-to-be. We're going to be married."

When I became conscious of my mouth hanging open, I closed it. "When did this happen?"

"Just last night. My train from Chicago got in last night in time for me to visit the hospital, and I popped the question. She gets released tomorrow, and we're getting married Saturday." He gave me a smug smile.

I went over and sat on one of the benches lining the mustering room walls. I needed to sit down. "Say it again, Harry. I don't think I heard it right."

"I said it three ways. Gladys and I are going to be married."

"Why?"

The smile disappeared from his face. "What you mean, why?"

I said carefully, "We're supposed to be friends, Harry, so I wouldn't insult the girl you mean to marry for the world. She strikes me as a pleasant gal, and she's certainly a beautiful one. But you gave some sworn testimony in court last week that doesn't quite jibe with this decision. I never before heard of a cop marrying a woman he'd arrested as a prostitute."

His face reddened. "Careful, Mike."

I said impatiently, "Don't try to sidetrack me with a chivalry act, Harry. I said I don't mean any insult to your fiancée. But you can't get away from your sworn testimony. Either you believed she was a prostitute, or deliberately perjured yourself."

"I don't have to explain to you why I'm getting married," he said angrily. "That's not police business."

"Did you perjure yourself?"

He started to get even more angry, then suddenly deflated. "No," he said in a sullen voice. "I thought she was when I testified, but I've changed my mind."

"Why?"

He looked at me for a long time. Finally he said reluctantly, "I'll sound like a jerk if I tell you."

"You sound like a jerk now. Maybe the explanation will make you sound better."

He tugged embarrassedly at an ear. "There's a little more to it than sounding like a jerk. You could get me suspended from the force if I told you the whole thing and you wanted to be nasty about it. There's a little matter of my getting drunk on duty."

"For cripes sake, Harry," I said. "I'm trying to crack a city-wide racket. I'm not interested in two-bit stuff like a cop being drunk on duty."

He tugged at his ear some more, looking more embarrassed by the minute. "Hell, Mike, it was all a mistake. I told the truth in Women's Court, except I condensed it a little. Remember when the judge asked me what 'Before you know it' consisted of, and I said it was just a figure of speech?"

I nodded.

"Well, actually we spent the whole afternoon together. I picked her up like I said, and at the time I thought she was a pro. But she didn't suggest her apartment until we'd had about a dozen drinks apiece in a half dozen bars. In fact I'm not sure I didn't make the suggestion instead of her. We were both a little boiled by them, and I know she told me she had this apartment, but maybe I was the one who suggested we go there. Things got pretty torrid at her place, and eventually she did undress, just as I testified. But it was because she liked me, Mike, not because she was trying to sell herself. I didn't know it at the time, but I do now. She meant it as a free offering."

"You swore under oath you asked her how much, and she said twenty-five dollars," I snapped at him.

"It was a joke, Mike. I did ask her, and she said twenty-five. But she thought I was joking, and she just quipped back in reply. Don't you see?"

I shook my head slowly. "No, I don't see at all."

"Listen," he said, not looking at me. "I was about half drunk. Drunk on duty, you understand. But I was still being a cop. I made the arrest in good faith. By the time the case came up, I was beginning to worry about it. But what was I going to do? Confess I was drunk and get kicked off the force? I wasn't sure I had made a mistake. I just thought I might have. That's why I was so nervous on the stand. That, and because I realized I liked the girl a hell of a lot. I testified to what had happened, but I wasn't at all sure I'd interpreted what had happened right. Now I know I didn't. Last night we got everything straightened out between us and found out we were in love. So we're going to get married."

I didn't know whether to believe him or not. It seemed an awfully sudden decision to marry. Besides, even if he was satisfied she wasn't a streetwalker, he knew from my questions in court that she was, or had been a call girl. And that still made her a prostitute.

I knew he was going to stick to the story, however, and there wasn't much point in trying to shake it.

Rising from the bench, I said wearily, "Well, accept my congratulations, Harry. Hope you're happy. I won't bother your future wife any more, but if she ever decides she'd like to talk to me, tell her I'd be glad to hear from her."

"I don't think she'll want to do that, Mike," he said in a firm voice. "That's a dead issue. We're going to start our life off clean, and not rake up a lot of stuff from the past."

That was that. My investigation of the call-girl racket had finally ground to a complete halt, with nowhere to go from there.

chapter eleven

FOR THE NEXT couple of weeks I did nothing whatever about the call-girl racket. It was still my baby, but I had come to a dead end, so I simply tabled it. Harry Allerup and his new wife were off on a two-week honeymoon during this period.

Then, just two weeks after my conversation with Harry Allerup, I got a phone call in the middle of the night. The ringing blasted me from a sound sleep, and I went through the motions of switching on my bedside lamp and groping for the alarm clock before I realized it was the phone ringing and not the clock.

I said sleepily, "Hello."

A feminine voice said, "Mr. Macauley?" The voice was completely empty, the voice of a woman who was dead inside.

"Yes," I said. "Who's this?"

"Gloria—Gladys Trask. I mean Gladys Allerup." She was in such a state of shock, she was having difficulty remembering her own name.

I glanced at the clock and saw it was three A.M. "What's the matter?" I asked sharply.

"They killed him." There was no emotion in her voice. It was a lifeless statement of fact.

"Who?" I said. "Harry?"

"Yes. He wouldn't listen to me. I told him—" Her voice trailed off hopelessly.

"Where are you?" I asked.

"At our new apartment. Thirteen twenty Gaylor." She emitted a sound similar to a laugh, but with no laughter in it. It was a wild, choking sound, on the verge of hysteria. "Our honeymoon flat."

Thirteen twenty Gaylor wasn't more than ten blocks from my place. "Be there in fifteen minutes," I said. "Stay there and don't touch anything."

I took about three minutes to dress, another two to race downstairs and get my car started, and about five to roar the ten blocks over to Gaylor. I shaved five minutes off the time I had told Gloria it would take.

Thirteen twenty Gaylor was a four-family flat with separate entrances to each apartment. Allerup's was the right-hand lower one. Gloria left the chain on when she opened to my ring, examining me from dead eyes until she was sure it was I. Then she slipped the chain and pulled the door wide. She was fully dressed and her long tawny hair was in perfect order, indicating she hadn't been to bed that night at all.

The place consisted of four rooms in the shape of a square, with a center hall. A bathroom and the stairs to the basement gave off the hall. Moving like a sleepwalker, she led me through the front room, into the hall and down the basement stairs. She hadn't even said hello. She just moved off and I followed.

The basement ran under the whole house and was apparently used by all four tenants, because four separate pairs of set tubs stood along one wall. Along another four hot-air furnaces were lined up. Someone, possibly Gloria, had turned on all the lights which could be controlled from her apartment. One burned over by the furnaces, another over a pair of the set tubs and a third at the bottom of the stairs.

When I saw what was left of Harry Allerup, an almost overpowering rage welled up in me. Harry had once been a friend of mine. Now he was nothing but a lump of bruised and battered flesh. He lay on his back near the set tubs, clad in nothing but blood-stained pajama bottoms. He had been beaten to death, beaten brutally and much more violently than Gloria had been. His face wasn't even identifiable. His body was a mass of welts and bruises and dents, the latter indicating places where bones had given way.

Only the fact that the senseless brutality of the crime put me into an overwhelming rage kept me from being sick all over the floor. The people who had done this were animals, not humans, and I wanted to get my hands on them so that I could crush them and watch them squirm and listen to their cries of agony as flesh gave way and bones cracked. They didn't deserve mere arrest and trial. They deserved the same treatment they handed out.

Gloria stood watching me dully, not looking at the thing that had been her husband. I knelt beside the body, not because I thought there was the slightest chance he was still alive, but because it's instinctive to make the useless gesture of checking pulse even on an obvious corpse.

This time there was no doubt. He had been dead for at least a couple of hours. Rigor mortis had begun to set in.

I rose again. "Let's go back upstairs," I suggested gently.

She moved toward the stairs like an automaton, led me up them and on into the front room. There she stood and gazed at me without expression, her face a complete blank. So far she hadn't said a word since I entered the apartment.

"What happened, Gloria?" I asked.

"I told him we shouldn't come back to this town," she said in a dead voice, more to herself than to me. "I told him they'd never let us quit, that they'd be too afraid one of us would talk. But he wouldn't listen. He thought we could turn straight and just forget the past."

The words sent a deep depression over me, for the only construction you could put on them was that Harry Allerup had been a crooked cop. You don't like to learn things like that about a dead friend.

"Was Harry a part of the call-girl racket?" I asked quietly.

"Of course," she said dully. "That's why he was killed. Because he wanted out."

"Killed by who, Gloria? Who beat him like that?"

"They did. The same ones who beat me. Which ones, I don't know. Some of Tupper Smith's goons."

"When did it happen?" I asked. "He's been dead for some time."

"I don't know," she said in the same dull tone. "I discovered him about two, but I'd been in the house about an hour by then. It took me another hour to get around to phoning you. I fainted and was out for a while. Then I just sat looking at nothing for a long time. I couldn't even think."

"You weren't here when it happened?"

She shook her head. "I went for a walk around midnight. I was nervous about coming back to town, and I couldn't sleep. I got up and left Harry sleeping and took a walk."

Suddenly she dropped her face into her hands and began to weep. "Oh God!" she whispered. "I left the latch off so I could get back in without a key. I left him defenseless with the door unlocked, so they could walk right in on him."

I thought that they probably had expected to find her too, but I didn't say it. She had enough troubles at the moment without having to think about her own body lying on the basement floor next to her husband's. Probably her decision to take a midnight walk was the only reason she was alive.

Once her tears started to flow, she let down the emotional bars and gave way to her grief. Collapsing on the sofa, she wept as though she could never stop. There wasn't any point in trying to soothe her. She needed the release of tears, so I let her cry herself out.

Eventually she wiped her eyes with a handkerchief, sniffed a couple of times and said in a small voice, "What am I going to do, Mr. Macauley?"

"Tell me as much as you can, I'll call Homicide, and then we'll get out of here. You won't want to stay here tonight."

"No," she agreed. "I couldn't stand that. I never want to see this place again."

She was a little calmer now, beyond hysteria and resigned to hopelessness. I got out of her that when she returned from her lonely walk about one A.M. and found Harry missing from bed, she at first assumed he'd awakened and had taken a walk too. She wandered through the house for a time, made and drank a cup of tea while awaiting his return, then restlessly wandered through it a second time. This time, as she passed through the hall, she spotted a crack of light under the basement door and opened it to investigate. Otherwise she might not have discovered her husband's body until the next day.

I went to the phone and called Homicide. Sergeant Johnny Sullivan was pulling the night trick on the desk, and I gave him a complete rundown. Johnny is a pot-bellied old-timer marking the days off to retirement, but a good cop. He said the boys would be over right away.

"I'm not going to stick around, Johnny," I said. "I'm going to get this girl out of here and hide her away. I think she's in danger of getting the same treatment her husband did. In fact I can't understand why they didn't wait around for her to return."

"Maybe they figured she was out of town," Johnny suggested. "Finding her husband in bed asleep like that. They wouldn't know she'd just gone for a walk."

"Yeah," I said. "That's probably it. Anyway I think she's in danger, so I'm going to hide her out."

"She's an important witness," he protested.

"She can't tell you anything I haven't already given you," I said. "Anyway, in case you've forgotten it, the function of the police is to collect evidence for the D.A., not just for their own information. And I've already questioned her."

I don't often pull rank, but what I told him was entirely true. In theory the district attorney's office is in charge of criminal cases from the instant they are reported, and the police function is merely to collect and preserve evidence so that the D.A. can prove in court what happened. In practice the D.A. sometimes doesn't even know a crime has been committed until the police complete the investigation and dump all the evidence in his lap. But I had full authority to direct the investigation in any way I chose.

Being a veteran officer, Johnny Sullivan knew this, and he didn't argue. "All right, Mike," he said agreeably. "Leave the door open then, so the boys can get in. You can let me know tomorrow where you've taken the girl."

chapter twelve

I TOOK GLORIA to the Acorn Inn Motel, which was on the edge of town but still inside the city limits, far enough from the center of things to be relatively safe, yet still within my jurisdiction. She made no objection when I registered her under the name of Mary Jones, but she looked a little puzzled. I told her why after I had carried her bag into the cabin.

"I think the same people who killed Harry will be looking for you too, Gloria. Probably your taking that walk saved your life. I want you to lie low here and don't let anyone in but me. Don't even go out for meals. I'll bring them to you personally."

She turned a little pale. "All right," she said in a low voice. "Whatever you say."

I glanced at my watch and saw it was now past four A.M. "Feel up to talking any more tonight?" I asked.

"I don't care," she said. "I couldn't sleep anyway. And I don't feel much like being alone."

While Gloria had been packing, I'd had the forethought to hunt down Harry Allerup's liquor supply and slip a bottle of bourbon into her bag. Now she got it out. There was no soda and no ice, but there were two glasses in the cabin. I made a pair of water highballs.

"What do you want to talk about?" she asked after sampling her drink.

"The call-girl racket," I said. "Don't you think it's about time you told me what you were going to before you got beat up?"

"It's too late to do any good now," she said in a colorless voice. "But maybe it will help you catch Harry's killers."

So finally I got the story I had been waiting weeks to hear. The wait had been worth it. With Gloria as a co-operative witness, I had enough evidence to take to the grand jury and get at least one indictment. An indictment against Tupper Smith for procuring. Gloria gave me names, dates and places she had met men through arrangements made by Smith. Her voice was bitter as she told the tale, and she made no attempt to conceal her own self-loathing at having sold her body for money.

"If you're willing to repeat that story on the stand, we'll put Mr. Smith away for some time," I said. "But he's only the front for the ring, isn't he? There must be others."

"There's the city part of the organization. The people who dig up customers. Tupper Smith just handles the girls. I don't know who the city contacts are, though. Then there's supposed to be some city official involved who would take the heat off things in case of trouble. I don't know who he is either. And there's Sheriff Merz."

"Merz?" I said eagerly. "What do you know about him?"

"Not much, really. I don't have any actual evidence that he's part of the ring, but he visits the farm regularly, and the girls are supposed to be nice to him. Free of charge."

This was interesting, but it only substantiated the belief I already had that Merz had a tie-in with the racket. It wasn't concrete evidence that he was guilty of accepting bribes.

I said, "You never saw any money pass between Smith and Merz?"

She shook her head. "It was generally supposed by all the girls that Smith paid him for protection. But I couldn't testify to it in court."

Our glasses were empty by then, so I rose and mixed two more drinks. When we were settled again, I said, "Now about this beating you took. Have any idea who did it?"

She shook her head again. "Only that it was ordered by Tupper Smith. When I told him I wanted out of the racket, he said sure, if I'd leave town and never return. He said it made him nervous to have reformed call girls around, because they had a habit of developing consciences about their pasts and going to the police. I told him I wouldn't do that, and he said he didn't accept promises. I could either leave town or be fixed up so that no man would even want me for free, let alone paying for me. That's when I phoned your office the first time. Before he threatened me, I didn't intend to turn him in. I just wanted to forget what I'd been and start my life over. But the threat frightened me. I thought maybe you'd give me some protection in return for talking."

"Then why did you change your mind?"

"Because of Harry. I met him right after my conversation with Tupper Smith. I didn't know it at the time, but he'd been assigned by the ring to keep an eye on me and make sure I didn't go to the police. I didn't know he was part of the racket, you see. I thought he was an honest cop. When I told him I'd 'phoned you, he talked me into not following up. He said he loved me and wanted to marry me, and he didn't like the idea of his future wife being the star witness in a sensational trial, where everyone in town would know she had been a call girl. So I dropped the idea. I guess the ring wasn't satisfied that I'd stay quiet, though, so they framed me on that streetwalking charge in an effort to shame me into leaving town."

"That was a deliberate frame, was it?" I asked. "Harry gave me a different story."

She flushed. "I know what he told you. He told me about it afterward. Actually I'd known Harry several weeks by then, and thought we were engaged. He'd never tried to touch me up until that day. Then we had a date at my place, he started making love to me, and when I gave in, he arrested me."

I looked at her in amazement. "Yet you still married him after treatment like that? I think he also was at least the indirect cause of your being beaten. He was in my office at the time you phoned, so he knew we were going to meet and where. I think he tipped off Tupper Smith as to where you were, and that you were going to talk."

Her eyes lowered to her glass. "I know," she said in a low voice. "But I loved him, and a woman in love can forgive almost everything. Oh, I hated him at first. But he was just following orders from the ring. When he came to see me at the hospital and said how sorry he was, and he now realized he really did love me, I had to forgive him. He said he wanted out of the racket too, and we'd start life over together."

I drained my glass and set it on the dresser. "Apparently Tupper Smith doesn't like reformed crooked cops around any more than he likes reformed call girls."

"I don't think it was Tupper Smith he was afraid of," she said quickly. "I think it was someone here in town. The official who was supposed to furnish protection in the city."

"But he never mentioned who that was?"

She shook her head. "I think it was someone in an important position, though. He just referred to him as the big boss."

I had thought we had a pretty clean town, but apparently there was at least one rotten apple in the barrel. Someone in an influential position too. The suspicion that there was such a person behind the scenes had been growing in me for some time, because of the invisible opposition I seemed to encounter from all directions in the call-girl investigation. This must be the person who had pulled strings to keep Harry Allerup out of my way for so long. Perhaps if I had Lieutenant Stan Spooner trace up through the chain of command to find out where the orders for Harry Allerup's leave and his trip to Chicago had originated, I could put the finger on this person.

A faint hunch as to who it might be entered my mind, but I didn't like the thought, so I pushed it out again.

I changed the direction of the conversation by asking abruptly, "How did Harry get along with your brother Sid?"

Gloria looked surprised at the question. "Why, all right."

"I asked because of something a girl named Penny Coynes said to me once. Know her?"

"Why, yes. She's a good friend of mine. She's one of the—"

When she stopped short, I said, "One of the call girls. I know it, so you're not giving your friend away. She said that Tupper Smith had a theory that it was Sid who beat you up, because he discovered you were a call girl."

She looked completely amazed. "My own brother? Sid wouldn't lay a hand on me. He might beat somebody else up for looking at me sidewise, but he wouldn't touch me. In fact, if he ever finds out who beat me, I think he'll kill them. He tries to protect me as though I was still a kid."

"Does he know you were a call girl?"

She flushed. "I guess. We never talked about it again after that night at the hospital, but I could tell by the way he acted he knew. He didn't know before that night, though. We always kept it from him because Sid has kind of old-fashioned ideas and—"

"Who's we?" I interrupted.

She looked confused. "I mean me. Nobody else."

She hadn't meant just herself, though. Apparently she had been in conspiracy with someone to conceal her call-girl activities from her brother, but didn't want me to know who. It didn't seem important, so I dropped it.

"You think Sid could possibly have beaten Harry? Because he resented your marriage, for instance."

"Oh, no," she said definitely. "He was glad about the marriage. I think he was beginning to regard me as a fallen woman, and was relieved that Harry was making me an honest one. Sid's crazy about me, Mr. Macauley. He'd never do anything to hurt me, and he knew I loved Harry. Sid would do anything for me."

By then it was pushing five in the morning and was already light. I decided I had about as much information as I could get from Gloria, so I left, first repeating my warning not to let anyone in the cabin except me.

chapter thirteen

IT WAS SIX by the time I got to bed, and the alarm went off two hours later. I'd had about three hours' sleep before Gloria's phone call at three A.M., however, so I didn't feel too bad.

I phoned Miss Rains that I'd be a little late to the office and drove out to the Acorn Inn Motel. En route I stopped for a bag of groceries to carry Gloria over until I could make better arrangements for her. There was a gas plate and a couple of pans in the cabin, enough cooking equipment to serve temporarily.

Gloria was still asleep, and I had to pound for some time before I could awaken her. When she finally came to the door, she wore a frilly white robe and her tawny hair was tousled. She was beautiful still half asleep, though. I could understand why Harry Allerup wanted her for a wife even after knowing her past.

I only stayed long enough to deliver the groceries and tell her I'd be back that evening. Then I drove over to police headquarters to see what had come of last night's investigation.

Nothing much had that I didn't already know. Johnny

Sullivan wasn't there because he was currently on the night trick, but I had the desk man pull the case folder and looked it over.

The time of Harry Allerup's death was estimated at between midnight and one A.M., which conformed to Gloria's story, and its immediate cause was a splintered rib puncturing the heart. He'd had a number of other injuries which might have caused death also, if the rib hadn't.

A lot of fingerprints had been lifted from the flat and the basement, and were still being processed. There had been no sign of forced entry, which again conformed to Gloria's story, as she'd said she left the door unlocked when she went for her walk. There had been no sign of struggle in the flat.

The theory was that Allerup's killers had surprised him in bed, forced him down to the basement, probably at gunpoint, and had methodically beaten him to death. It was assumed the basement had been chosen so that sounds of the beating would be less likely to be heard in the other flats.

No one had heard any disturbance. All the other tenants had been interviewed, plus the neighbors on either side. A further check of other neighbors along the street was planned for that day, to see if anyone recalled seeing the killers' car.

The rest of that day I was tied up in matters having nothing to do with the call-girl racket. When I left the office at five, I decided to check on Gloria again before dinner.

Then, as I started to drive toward the motel, another thought occurred to me. I really needed help to protect Gloria, for it was a full-time bodyguarding chore, and all I could do was periodically check to see if she was still safe. What was needed was someone who could be with her constantly.

I didn't want to ask for police protection, because that would involve having all of officialdom know where she was. Which almost certainly meant the information would seep up to the man Harry Allerup had referred to as the "big boss."

My conversation with Gloria the previous night had convinced me there was one person I could trust her with at any rate. Her brother, Sid Trask.

Penny Coynes had mentioned that Sid Trask was the yard manager at Sullivan's Lumber Company. I knew that was just off Lincoln Avenue, in the same general area as the textile factories, and not much out of my way en route to the Acorn Inn Motel. I decided to stop there on the off chance that Trask might still be around after five.

The Sullivan Lumber Company consisted of a small glass-fronted store where customers did their ordering, and a number of large sheds for the storage of lumber. The latter, plus several piles of lumber out in the open, were enclosed by a high board fence which had a gate in it for trucks to go in and out. The store was closed for the day, but since the truck gate stood open, I assumed someone was still in the yard.

Leaving my car parked on the street, I walked through the truck gate. It took me only moments to check the aisles between the several piles of outdoor lumber and decide no one was in the yard itself. I began to search the sheds.

I found Sid Trask in the second one I checked. This was an open-air shed about sixty feet long with no sides. A roof held up by supporting poles protected the stored lumber from rain.

Apparently the yard manager was taking inventory. He stood on the back of a platform truck counting the pieces in an enormous pile of two-by-fours and entering data in a small notebook. He was in denim overalls, heavy shoes and no hat. His back was to me when I entered the place.

I called up to him, "Hey, Trask!"

He swung around, his face darkened and he snapped the notebook closed. Thrusting it into his pocket, he dropped from the truck platform to the ground with remarkable agility for such a large man.

Balling fists on his hips, he said, "What the hell do you want? Another lesson?"

I had come with the intention of forgetting the incident in my hallway, because I needed the man as an ally. But since he brought the subject up, I wasn't going to pussyfoot around it.

I said, "You couldn't give me one when I was looking, you overgrown ape."

That effectively postponed further conversation. He didn't give me a chance to inform him that his sister was a widow and needed his protection. He stepped forward and his left fist lashed out at my face.

It was a fast-moving blow, but this time I was prepared

for it. I shifted my head an inch to let it whistle past my jaw. He was still off balance when I drove a right into his stomach with all the power of my shoulder behind it.

It was like smashing my fist against a wall. That blow should have doubled him over in agony, but he only grunted. It did me more damage than him, for it nearly paralyzed my shoulder.

I ducked his counter-punch and threw a couple of light left jabs into his face to keep him off balance until the numbness disappeared from my right arm. The jabs irritated him and he bulled in with his arms spread to envelop me in a bear hug. This left him wide open for left and right hooks to the jaw that cracked like pistol shots.

He just blinked and kept coming.

I sank another right into his solar plexus, but then his big hands had me by the shoulders. Before he could draw me against his chest to crush me with his powerful arms, I threw myself backward, taking him with me. As my back hit the dirt, I drove both feet into his stomach and heaved upward. He did a neat flip and landed on his back.

We bounced erect simultaneously.

"You like judo, huh?" he panted, and threw a body block at my feet.

I tried to sidestep, but wasn't quite fast enough. His shoulder hit my shins and tumbled me forward. I landed on my hands, tucked my head into my chest and did a gymnasium tumble which bounced me erect again a half dozen feet away from him. He bounced to his feet at the same instant.

Now I had a pile of lumber to my back, and there was nowhere to go when he rushed me with both arms flailing. I blocked a left with a forearm, ducked a right, then caught a second left flush on the chin.

The blow nearly tore my head off. It also made me sore enough to forget science. I stood toe-to-toe with him and slugged it out.

I had twice his speed, but he had twice my power. I landed two blows to his one, but they didn't seem to affect him, while his had the effect of being hit with a baseball bat. I was tasting blood from a split lip and could feel an eye beginning to swell before he showed the first sign of damage. Then, suddenly, blood was spurting from his nose.

I had been getting discouraged about ever being able to

hurt him when the blood appeared. The sight of it threw me into a frenzy of renewed effort. I drove him backward with a flurry of blows until he stopped and brought one up from the ground to explode under my chin. I staggered backward, bounced off the lumber pile and felt myself slipping into blackness. In a final desperate effort I brought around a looping right which caught him flush on the button.

It was the last blow I was capable of throwing. I stood staring at him stupidly, my arms hanging limply at my sides, fighting unconsciousness and stoically waiting for the *coup de grace.*

It didn't come. Gradually I realized he was gazing at me just as stupidly, swaying on his feet in an effort to stay erect.

I lurched forward, fell against him and we went down together in an exhausted heap.

chapter fourteen

AFTER A WHILE things stopped spinning and I developed enough energy to climb to my feet. I reeled over to the lumber pile and kept from falling again by holding on to one end of it. Sid Trask pushed himself to hands and knees and wagged his head back and forth in an effort to clear it.

Looking at him, I decided if I looked as bad as he did, I was a mess. His lower lip was puffed, one eye was half closed, and there was a steady drip-drip of blood from his nose. I felt of my own split lower lip, then tenderly probed the swelling about my eye.

"Want to go another round?" I asked in a voice I meant to make strong, but which came out in an exhausted whisper. "Or would you rather call it a draw?"

He stared up at me and shook his head a few more times. "Let's call it a draw this time," he said huskily.

When I finally got my sea legs back, I helped him to his feet. Supporting each other like a couple of drunks, we staggered to the back door of the store, inside and over to a washroom. Liberal applications of cold water helped recovery to the point where we could both stand without swaying.

Sid Trask led the way out of the washroom, leaned his rump against the store's counter and gazed at me. "You're the only guy who ever knocked me down, Macauley," he said. "And I used to fight in the ring."

"I'm glad you're past your prime," I told him. "One more tap on the jaw and I'd still be sleeping."

"I must be slipping," he said in a morose voice. "I need a couple of workouts. Did you want anything with me except a battle?"

"Don't you read the newspapers?" I asked.

He gave me a blank look. "I haven't seen one today."

There wasn't any gentle way to break it, so I gave it to him cold. "Your brother-in-law was beaten to death last night."

He drew in his breath sharply. "Harry?"

"Harry," I said. "In the basement of his apartment house. Probably your sister would be dead too, if she'd been home at the time. She had gone for a midnight walk, and it saved her life. But I think she's still in danger. I have her hidden at a motel."

"What motel?"

"The Acorn Inn out at the edge of town. I came by here to get you to help me protect her."

Without a word he walked back into the washroom. Within three minutes he was back, wearing a suit in place of his overalls.

"Let's go," he said.

On the way to the motel I told him everything I knew about the killing. When I finished, he said, "So the police haven't any idea who did it, huh? Do you?"

"Allerup was part of the call-girl racket. He wanted out. It seems pretty obvious the gang was afraid he might talk. He was beaten for the same reason your sister was. Because he wanted to reform."

His face darkened and I said, "You're going to have to face it that your sister was a call girl. If that makes you mad, we'll stop the car and go another round. But it's the truth. If you want her to stay alive, you have to face it. It's the call-girl bunch that's after her. You won't make a very effective bodyguard if you refuse to believe in the people who want to kill her."

He didn't say anything for the rest of the trip.

Apparently Gloria—or Gladys—had been crying shortly before we arrived, for her eyes were red-rimmed. She started again the moment she saw her brother. He took her into his arms and patted her shoulder as though she were an infant.

"It's all right now, Sis," he said. "Nothing more's going to happen to you. I'm taking care of you from here on in."

When the girl stopped crying and settled down enough to listen, we held a council of war. It was decided the motel cabin wasn't suitable as a permanent hideout for a couple of reasons. It wasn't safe enough in case Tupper Smith's goons started a systematic check of motels in their hunt for the girl, and it was too confining. What was needed was a hiding spot the gang couldn't find, and one which would allow Gloria some movement.

Gladys herself solved the problem. "How about Harry's river cottage?" she asked.

I remembered that Harry Allerup had such a place, because that was where he had spent his leave. "Know where it is?" I asked.

She nodded. "We spent part of our honeymoon there. It's only about thirty-five miles out."

I frowned. "In Sheriff Merz's territory?"

"No. The other way out of town. In Black County."

I said dubiously, "Thirty-five miles is pretty far for me and your brother to run back and forth. And we'd want to keep a pretty constant check on you."

Trask said, "Why couldn't she phone us every so often, so we'd know she was okay?"

"There's no phone at the cottage," Gladys said. "There's a little town about four miles from the cottage, though. If I had a car, I could phone in from there."

I shook my head. "Too dangerous. I don't want you appearing in public at all."

"I've got it," Trask said. "I'll get my girl friend to stay with her. Alice has a car, and she could drive into town and do the phoning."

I wasn't too enthusiastic about this. From my one glimpse of Alice Dill at the hospital I got the impression that she was strictly the cafe-society type. She didn't strike me as the sort of girl who would be satisfied to sit in a lonely river cottage for any length of time without any men around.

I was getting along with Sid Trask too well to want to

start another argument, however. I kept my mouth shut, and he interpreted my silence as agreement.

Strangely, I got the impression Gloria wasn't too happy at the thought of having Alice as her sole companion at the cottage either. Not because of anything she said, because she made no objection. But there was an odd look of reluctance on her face when her brother made the suggestion. It struck me as peculiar because at the hospital I had gotten the impression that the two women were good friends.

It was decided that we would all drive to Alice Dill's place in my car, Sid Trask would go in to help her pack while we waited outside, then he and Alice would follow Gloria and me to the cottage.

Alice Dill's apartment was on Hempstead, one of the top residential sections in town, which seemed to indicate she had money. While Gloria and I were waiting outside in the car, I asked her what Alice did.

She didn't answer for a time. Then she said, "Nothing, if you mean work. She has an independent income."

We had about a twenty-minute wait before a yellow convertible pulled up alongside of us and its horn honked. Alice Dill was behind the wheel and Sid Trask sat next to her. Apparently she kept the car garaged behind the apartment house.

I waved her on so that I could get out of my parking place, then passed her and led the way. Gloria told me to take Rivershore Drive north of town as far as Titusgrove. We stopped at a roadhouse just short of Titusgrove, and after I had checked it to make sure no one was there who might recognize Gloria, we went in and had dinner, as by now it was nearing eight o'clock.

It was eight-forty-five by the time we reached Harry Allerup's river cottage. Because of daylight saving it still wasn't quite dark, though, and in the fading light we could make out the scene well enough.

The cottage was situated in a bend of the river, so that it was surrounded by water on three sides. Like most places along the Missouri it was built on stilts because of the annual spring floods. The stilts had been boarded over on two sides to form a double car port, open at either end, and from inside this a wooden flight of stairs led upward to the cottage itself.

There were only three rooms in the place. The stairs led

into the main room, which took up half the space of the cottage. This was a combination kitchen, dining room and living room, with a stove, sink, icebox, eating table, a worn sofa and a couple of easy chairs. The other two rooms were bedrooms.

As there was nothing along the river here between Titusgrove and Clement except a few summer cottages, there was no utility service. A hand pump over the sink was the only source of water, which came from a deep well beneath the cottage. The kitchen stove used bottled gas. And light was furnished by Coleman lanterns in each of the rooms. The icebox was the old-fashioned kind with a compartment for ice in top. Gloria said that there was an ice house in the small town of Clement, four miles away, where they could buy ice.

Sid Trask gave the redheaded Alice Dill final instructions before he and I started back to town.

"You drive into Clement to phone either me or Mr. Macauley twice a day," he said. "About noon, and again after supper. Nobody could find you way out here, but we want to be sure."

"Sure, honey," she said, but she was eyeing me when she said it.

I don't know why, but I felt uneasy about driving off and leaving the two women alone. Alice Dill seemed too much of a party girl, and I wondered how dependable she was. She might get bored by the lack of bright lights and go touring the bars of Clement or Titusgrove in search of congenial people to bring back for a party.

I said, "Remember, we don't want anyone at all to know Gladys is here, Alice. So if you run into anyone you know in Clement, don't drop any invitations."

She looked at me with raised eyebrows. "What do you mean, Mr. Macauley? I don't know anyone out this way."

I didn't elaborate. I just left it there. A few minutes later Sid Trask and I started the drive back to town.

chapter fifteen

I CHECKED WITH HOMICIDE again the next morning, but there was nothing new on the Allerup kill. All the prints found at the murder scene had been checked out as being made either by the dead man, his wife, or neighbors who had recently been in the flat. Furthermore, no one in the area had been turned up who either heard sounds of the beating, or noticed any suspicious persons around.

Johnny Sullivan was still on the night trick, but he had left word with the day crew to ask me when I was going to bring Allerup's widow down to headquarters for questioning. I said never, that I would produce her when I was ready for a grand-jury indictment, but meantime she was staying under wraps. I suggested that if Sullivan wanted some specific information from her, he could tell me what it was and I'd relay it on to her and relay her answers back to him.

The boys at Homicide didn't like this much, but there really wasn't much they could do about it, because technically the police investigate crimes under the direction of the D.A.'s office. She was my witness, not Homicide's, and if I didn't want to I didn't have to let her talk to anyone until the day I put her on the stand before a grand jury.

When I left Homicide I decided I might as well drop in on Lieutenant Stan Spooner as long as I was at police headquarters anyway. I found the round-faced Morals Division chief up to his neck in paper work, but he pushed it aside when I entered his office.

"Sit down, Mike," he said in his usually pleasant way. Then his expression turned a little morose. "Devil of a thing about Harry Allerup, wasn't it?"

I took a seat and lighted a cigarette. "Because he's dead, or because he turned out to be a crooked cop?"

"Both," Spooner said seriously. "The commissioner called a staff meeting this morning. It was hard to tell what he was most upset about—a cop being murdered, or the suggestion that he was crooked. He put the lid on that point until all the facts are in. He said if there's a leak to the papers about Harry's tie-in with the call-girl setup before he gives the word, some heads are going to fall."

I said, "I suppose that's smart. The man's dead, so he can hardly be kicked off the force. About all a news release would do would be tip off the call-girl ring that we knew about Harry's connection with it, and possibly start an editorial campaign for a department shakeup. There's not much doubt that Harry was part of the racket, though. He admitted it to his wife."

Stan Spooner shook his head gloomily. "It makes you wonder about human nature, doesn't it? I would have sworn Harry Allerup was a straight cop. The guy worked under me and was a personal friend of mine. You know, Mike, when I read Homicide's resume of the case, it shook me up more to learn he'd been a crooked cop than it did to realize he was dead."

"He was a friend of mine, too," I said.

The lieutenant stared at the window without seeing the traffic passing outside. After a time he looked at me again and said, "I noticed by the case report that you have Harry's widow under wraps. Where you hiding her, Mike?"

I shook my head. "I'll produce her when I'm ready to have her appear before a grand jury. Until then I wouldn't tell my own mother."

He raised his eyebrows. "You don't even trust us cops any more?"

"Harry Allerup was a cop," I said reasonably. "And he was part of the ring. There's another member of it somewhere in our official family too. Maybe the brains of the whole deal. Harry's wife says he referred to him as the 'big boss.' "

Stan Spooner raised his eyebrows again. "Any idea who it is?"

"Only that it's somebody with influence. I think somebody was pulling strings to keep me from seeing Allerup before he got married. First he got sent on leave, then on detached service to Chicago. Where'd those orders originate, Stan?"

The lieutenant looked blank. "Originate? Why the leave was routine, Mike. Harry requested it, he had time coming, so I approved it and sent it on to the chief of detectives, Mark Towner. I haven't checked, but I assume Mark gave it routine approval, it went on up to the chief of police, and the order was cut."

I thought this over and decided it led nowhere. Almost anyone might have suggested to Allerup that he apply for leave in order to avoid a session with me, but that didn't necessarily mean any of the officials whose approval was necessary had made the suggestion.

"How about the order for him to go to Chicago after a prisoner?" I asked.

"The chief of detectives just glooped him off. Captain Towner keeps a kind of duty roster for detached service, and pulls a man from one division one time, another the next. It was the Morals Division's turn when Harry was sent off."

I leaned forward to punch out my cigarette in his desk ash tray. "Do me a favor, will you, Stan? Feel out Captain Towner and find out if anyone specifically suggested Allerup for that trip."

"Why sure, Mike. You think that might lead you to this so-called big boss?"

"It might."

"You don't even have a hint as to who it might be?"

I shook my head.

"Has anyone in an official position been trying to side-track you from the call-girl investigation?"

I opened my mouth and closed it again. Sunshine Sever had thrown a couple of roadblocks in my way, but I was reasonably certain his motive had been inter-agency harmony rather than cover-up. Besides, it didn't make sense for him to have appointed me to break the call-girl racket if he himself was its head.

Except that he'd had to appoint someone. With the Citizens' Committee for Good Government screaming for action, he didn't have much choice.

You don't voice suspicions against your own boss with nothing more tangible to back you up than an uneasy feeling, though. I said, "Sheriff Merz has done his best to side-track me. But I doubt that he has enough influence in the city to get a detective sent to Chicago. This is somebody local."

Stan Spooner smiled slightly. "I heard about your clash with Merz. Did he really throw you out of his office bodily?"

I stared at him, then laughed. "That story must have come from the big windbag himself. He ordered me out when I called him a crook, I suggested he toss me out personally, and he called a deputy to do it for him. The deputy wasn't any braver than the sheriff. I walked out under my own power, and when I was good and ready."

Spooner's smile widened. "See how rumors grow? I heard you went out nose first, with the sheriff's foot helping you along."

I might have expected Sheriff Merz to spread a story like that. Not that I particularly cared if he wanted to salve his ego by telling people how tough he was.

I said, "He's tied in hand in glove with this call-girl racket, Stan. If he wasn't protected by the county line, I'd have you pull in both him and Tupper Smith, and we'd crack this thing wide open."

Stan Spooner nodded sympathetically. "He *is* protected by the county line though, Mike. And you know how long I'd have my job if I took a raiding party across the line."

"Yeah," I said. "About as long as I'd have mine for suggesting it. That damned line is like an official wall to bump my head on every time I make a move. I *know* the call-girl ring beat up Gloria Townsend and murdered Harry Allerup. I *know* Tupper Smith and Sheriff Merz run the county end of the racket. But I can't even bring them in for questioning, because they're outside my jurisdiction. Legally all I can do is ask Merz to question Smith. Which would make as much sense as asking a bank robber to take over the official investigation of his partner in crime."

"I know what you're up against," the lieutenant said. "I'm in the same boat. I'm supposed to suppress things like this call-girl ring, but what can I do when it operates from out of town? I'm stopped cold before I start. Even if I had some way to find out when a girl was meeting a date, all I could do is arrest the girl. I couldn't touch the ringleaders as long as they stay out of the city."

Rising, I shook my head. "You're not cheering me up much, Stan. All we're doing is weeping on each other's shoulders. I'm going back to the office and bask under my boss' sunny smile."

The District Attorney was beaming his ray of sunshine when I walked into his office. He greeted me as though we'd been separated for years instead of for a little over an hour. As this was often a prelude to bad news, I braced myself.

It wasn't long in coming. After a little inconsequential chit-chat he said casually, "Homicide wants to know why you're keeping as important a witness as Mrs. Allerup from them, Mike. I just got a call from Mark Towner."

"The chief of detectives? What's he got to do with Homicide?"

"Well, I guess they registered the complaint with him so it would come to me from a little higher up than a mere lieutenant. Why are you hiding her, Mike?"

"Because I think she's in danger," I said hotly. "Technically this office is responsible for investigation of crimes, Sunshine. The police are merely our agents. I have no responsibility to turn a witness over ot Homicide if I don't want to."

"Not technically," he conceded. "But they're experts at investigation, Mike. We'd be in a sad fix if they told us to do *all* our own investigation."

It was inter-agency peace he was worried about again. I ended the argument by saying in a definite tone, "They aren't going to get her, Sunshine. If you insist on it, you can have my resignation right now. But I still won't tell you where she is."

He knew when I couldn't be pushed another inch, and he gave in gracefully. "All right, Mike. Handle it the way you think best. I'll stall off Mark Tower."

As I started out the door, I stopped and said, "Heard anything more from Sheriff Merz?"

He shook his head. "Not since his written complaint about you."

"I just heard that he booted me out of his office that day. Literally."

Sunshine gave me a benign smile. "I hadn't heard that rumor yet, but I suppose I will if it's going around. He probably should have. I've had the urge myself more than once."

I grinned at him and went back to my own office.

chapter sixteen

AT NOON I GOT a phone call from Sid Trask, who said Alice Dill had phoned him from Clement, as instructed, to report everything okay. He said she had promised to call him at home again about seven.

I said, "You won't be able to reach me either here or at home at that time. Suppose I phone you about seven-fifteen?"

"All right," he said, and gave me his home phone number.

I wasn't going to be home at seven because I had plans for the evening. Plans which combined both business and pleasure. When the office closed at five, I drove over to Stoyle's Department Store.

As the stores in town stay open till five-thirty, I made it in plenty of time. A few of the counters were already covered by dust protectors, but customers were still at many of them. I took the elevator to the fourth floor and asked a clerk the way to the women's wear department.

One or two female customers still lingered here, but apparently they were through shopping and were merely waiting for packages. When a smartly-dressed floor lady asked what I wanted, I said I was looking for Miss Coynes.

"She's in the locker room getting ready to go home," she said. "She'll be out in a minute."

A few minutes later Peggy Coynes appeared, dressed for the street in a bright summer print that caressed her figure like the kiss of a lover. Today her hair was fixed in a pony tail tied with a red ribbon instead of in a sophisticated upsweep, and she looked about sixteen years old. When she saw me she stopped stock still, looking a little breathless.

I said, "Hello, Peggy."

She smiled then, but the breathless look stayed with her. "I'm glad you called me that, Mike. Instead of Penny."

"I told you when I came to take you to dinner it would be as Peggy the dress model," I reminded her.

"Oh, are we going to dinner?"

71

"Even angels have to eat, don't they?" I asked, and steered her toward the elevator.

Peggy wanted me to take her home first, for the feminine reason of changing her dress. As it looked like an entirely adequate dress to me, I gave her an argument.

"But I wore this to work this morning," she protested. "No girl wants to go out to dinner in the same dress she's worn all day."

"You've been modeling dresses all day, haven't you?" I pointed out. "You only had that dress on long enough to get to work."

I lost the argument, as men always lose such arguments to women. She had a small apartment on Mercer Street, and I waited in the front room while she not only made a complete change, but first took a shower.

She looked lovely when she finally came from the bedroom, but she had looked just as lovely before she went in. She wore another print dress, this one rose and white and of a simple cut which made it appropriate both for afternoon and evening. It was too hot for a dinner gown, so the only concession she made to the time of day was a small white evening bag.

Remembering that Peggy didn't care to be seen in public with me because of her fear that it might leak back to Tupper Smith that she was consorting with someone from the D.A.'s office, I took her to a place where I was reasonably certain neither of us would be recognized. I took her to the Coal Hole, an off-beat restaurant and bar on the east side of town. It was in the basement of an old brownstone house, the upper part of which had been converted into a cocktail lounge. The dining room was dimly lit by candles, so that it was difficult to see the other customers. A Turk named Ali Taj ran the place, and his cooking was wonderful. His prices matched the cuisine, which is why I wasn't known there.

I ordered two steaks, medium rare, and two martinis to precede them.

"This is nice, if it's purely social," Peggy said when the drinks were before us. "It's even nice if you're only after more information."

"I wouldn't pass up any information," I admitted. "But I've been planning to take you to dinner anyway. We'd be right here now even if the case was already cracked."

She made a face at me. "I'll believe that when you bring

me here again after it is cracked." Then her face grew serious. "You mean the call-girl investigation, don't you?"

"That and Harry Allerup's murder."

Her eyes widened. "Was that part of it, Mike?"

"It wasn't in the papers," I said, "but Harry Allerup was a member of the ring. Didn't you know that?"

She shook her head wonderingly. "Gloria didn't either. I'm sure she didn't. She used to tell me about him right after they met. How wonderful he was, and what a smart cop, and how glad she was she'd stopped being a call girl before she met him. She'd already quit then, you know, though Tupper Smith was giving her a hard time about it. I remember the day Gloria told me she'd confessed her past to Harry, and how I told her I thought that was a mistake. She said she couldn't marry him under false pretenses, and he had a right to know. Apparently he didn't confess his past to her, though, because she had no idea he was involved in the racket."

"She knew it before they finally got married," I told her. "They started out clean. He was getting out of the racket too, which is why he died. The ring doesn't like its employees to reform. It's afraid they'll get too much religion and start to talk."

Peggy turned a little pale. In a low voice she said, "I want to quit too, Mike. And I'm afraid."

"Have you said anything to Smith about quitting?" I asked quickly.

She shook her head. "No. But I've begged off every weekend since the one I was with you. Once I said I was sick, once that a friend had died in St. Louis and I had to go to the funeral and once—well, I used an excuse women can always use. He hasn't said anything, but I think he suspects I want to quit."

"You really serious about it?" I asked.

"Oh yes, Mike," she said earnestly. "I wish I'd never gotten involved. But I'm afraid of what happened to Gloria. And now to Harry Allerup. I don't think Tupper Smith will accept another excuse."

"Then don't give him any more," I said. "It's too dangerous. Check in for work as usual this weekend."

She gave me a strange look, a mixture of surprise and disappointment.

"You won't have to go on any dates," I explained. "I'll

have a friend of mine named Stacy phone in every Friday afternoon for a while and ask for you specifically. You can pretend to go out on dates, later pay Smith his fifty-dollar cut. I'll stake you to a cut."

Hope grew in her eyes, then she looked doubtful. "That would cost you fifty dollars a week."

"I think I'll have the ring smashed before too many more weeks. I can stand a hundred or two."

Hope flamed up again. "Would you, Mike? I'll pay you back. Every cent you spend."

"Maybe I can bill the city for it after the ring is smashed," I said. "Buying protection for a material witness should be a legitimate investigation expense."

By then our glasses were empty and the waiter came over to ask if we wanted refills. When he told us the steaks would be another quarter hour I ordered two more martinis. When he moved off again, I glanced at my watch, saw it was now seven-fifteen and rose from my seat.

"I have to make a phone call," I said. "Excuse me a minute."

chapter seventeen

SID TRASK ANSWERED the phone at once when I dialed. He said Alice Dill had just called again, and everything was quiet at the river cottage.

"How long is Gladys going to have to stay holed up there?" he asked.

"Until I have the people who killed Harry behind bars. I'm hoping that won't be long."

"It's kind of tough on the two girls," he said dubiously. "There's nothing much for them to do out there."

So Alice had registered a complaint against the inaction, I thought. "It would be tougher if Harry's killers caught up with your sister," I told him. "Better get it across to your girl friend that this is no game. It's a matter of life and death."

"Oh, Alice will stick it out all right," he said a little defensively. "She just wondered how long it would drag on."

I told him I couldn't say.

Our waiter had underestimated the time it would take for our steaks, I discovered when I got back to the table. They had already arrived. We pushed aside our second martinis untouched and started on the steaks instead.

It wasn't until we reached the coffee course that I returned to our former subject. I said, "If you want to get out of this mess fast, Peggy, you're going to have to cooperate. You willing to tell me everything you know about the racket?"

She nodded her head emphatically. "I'll help any way I can, Mike. But there isn't much I can tell you except how the business operates. I don't know a thing about Gloria's beating or Harry's murder."

Apparently she didn't either, for she couldn't give me a thing Gloria hadn't already given me. Her testimony in court would substantiate Gloria's in convicting Tupper Smith of procuring, but she had no more concrete evidence to offer of Sheriff Merz's complicity than the other girl had. Although, like Gloria, she said it was generally supposed among the girls that Merz received a regular payoff, she had no proof of it. And you can't take mere suspicion into court.

She also had no idea who the man Allerup referred to as the "big boss" might be. Which wasn't surprising inasmuch as she hadn't even known until I told her that Allerup himself had been part of the ring.

Finally I said, "I'd like to get a look at Smith's farm, Peggy. Willing to direct me out there?"

When she looked a little frightened, I said, "I won't get you in trouble. I'll leave you in the car and do my prowling alone. I just want you to show me where it is."

"All right," she decided. "I said I'd do anything I could to help."

It was a fine night for a ride along the river road. Every so often a break in the trees to our right brought us a glimpse of the Missouri, its muddy waters magically turned to silver by a nearly full moon. The air was balmy with the odor of summer growth, and there was just enough breeze to make the hot night comfortable.

With a lovely blonde at my side, it seemed a shame to waste the moon. I was almost tempted to find a parking spot somewhere in view of the river and devote the evening to romance. Then I thought of Gloria and Alice Dill out at the river cottage on the opposite side of town and wrenched my mind back to business.

Peggy broke a prolonged silence by saying, "Smith keeps a dog that roams the farm at night. A big, overgrown boxer. I'll have to take you past Fang."

I glanced sidewise at her. "Fang?"

"It's a fierce name," she said, "but he's really a friendly mutt. Boxers have such loose lips, they sometimes leave a tooth protruding when they close their mouths. When Fang does that, he looks like he's snarling, which is how he got his name. He's trained to bark at strangers, but to pass all us girls and certain other people. Such as Sheriff Merz, for instance. I'll have to introduce you to him, or he'll raise everybody on the place."

I thought that it was a good thing I hadn't tried to make a visit to the farm on my own, in view of the news that it was protected by a canine sentry.

I knew approximately where Tupper Smith's farm was because I knew that R.F.D. Two was Rivershore Drive. But as I had never been to the place, I didn't know its exact location. We rolled past the army of billboards and the drive-in theater I had passed the day I drove to the Lagoon to meet Gloria Townsend, passed the same two roadhouses I had noted that day when I was searching for the Lagoon, then finally passed the Lagoon.

I wasn't terribly surprised when Peggy told me to start slowing down only a half mile beyond the Lagoon. I had suspected all along that the farm wasn't far from the roadhouse where Gloria had taken her beating, and that the beaters had probably come from it.

Peggy started studying the roadside after telling me to slow, searching for familiar landmarks. Finally she said, "It's the lane to the left just ahead."

I slowed almost to a crawl, raised my highway lights as we passed the place and saw a lone roadside mailbox standing there with the name "Smith" painted on it in large black letters. The farm was on the opposite side of the road from the river, and apparently the house and barn were set well back, for no buildings of any sort were visible from the road.

A hundred yards beyond I made a U-turn, drove back

toward the lane and pulled onto the shoulder a dozen yards before reaching it.

"Better case me on the setup before we get out," I suggested. "I don't want to walk into Tupper Smith's arms."

"Well, the farmhouse and a barn and a couple of other buildings are up the lane about a hundred yards," Peggy said. "There aren't any outside guards except Fang, so you shouldn't walk into anybody's arms. There will probably be two or three girls in the house waiting for calls, plus Tupper Smith and his handyman, Matty Grange. He does odd jobs around the place and also chauffeurs the girls into town when they have dates. Then maybe a friend or two of Smith's will be here. Somebody like Merz or one of his deputies. A few men who are close to Smith come out here to see the girls. He doesn't allow mere customers to do that, though. They have to meet the girls in town."

"Is there a Mrs. Smith?" I asked.

Peggy shook her head. "He's a bachelor."

I got out of the car, walked around it and held the other door open for Peggy. Together we walked to the entrance of the lane. We stopped there and looked up it, but could see nothing in the moonlight but the empty lane stretching ahead of us.

Peggy took a deep breath. "Let's go. Fang should meet us before we get very far."

We started up the lane. We had gone perhaps twenty yards when a tan wraith slid from the underbrush and took up a crouched stance in front of us. It was one of the biggest boxers I ever saw, with a huge head and a chest like a barrel. He didn't growl or snarl, but he was tensed to leap in case he decided we weren't authorized visitors. His eyes glowed like twin embers in the moonlight.

"It's all right, Fang," Peggy said in a soothing voice, unhesitatingly walking up to the dog and laying a hand on his big head.

Instantly Fang's stub of a tail began to wag, and he shot out an enormous tongue to lap at her hand. She roughed up his ears, then pointed to me and said, "This is Mike, Fang. A friend of mine."

It was the first time I had ever been formally introduced to a dog. I said, "Hello, Fang," and the dog came over to sniff at my shoes. Cautiously I dropped my hand on his head and scratched between his ears. He wagged his tail.

"He'll be all right now," Peggy said. "He may follow you around, but he won't bark now that you've been introduced. Just don't let Tupper Smith spot you when Fang's around, though. He'd attack anyone, including me, that Smith sicked him on."

"I don't plan to let anyone spot me," I told her. "Better go back and wait in the car now."

"All right, Mike." She turned back in the direction from which we had come, then halted for a moment. "Be careful, Mike," she said in a low voice.

When she was out of sight, I started back up the lane. Fang chummily fell in at my side.

As Peggy had told me, the farmhouse, a barn and a couple of other outbuildings were clustered into a loose square about a hundred yards from the road. The moonlight made it bright enough to see everything clearly, and through the open door of the barn I could see a sedan parked inside. Three more automobiles stood in the yard, one bearing the official seal of the Sheriff's Department.

It looked as though I had picked a good time to come calling.

I walked toward the house quietly, but with no attempt at concealment. Except for some low underbrush alongside the lane, there was nothing to hide behind, and I decided that if anyone spotted me in the moonlight, I would merely say I was driving north and had stopped to ask directions.

No one challenged me, though. The house was of two stories, a rambling frame building with a porch running clear across its front and along one side. I circled the building warily, noting that there were lights in all three of the downstairs rooms and in one of the upstairs bedrooms. The shades were raised in all the downstairs windows, and only lace curtains covered them.

Fang lost interest in me by the time I had made a complete circuit of the house. When some small nocturnal animal made a rustling noise in the underbrush lining the lane, he was off like a shot to investigate it, disappearing as silently as he had appeared.

Quietly I went up the porch steps and moved to a front-room window.

chapter eighteen

THE LACE CURTAINS in the window were parted slightly, but I didn't put my face to the aperture. I could see well enough through the gauzy material without taking the chance of being spotted by those inside. Two young women sat in the front room, boredly watching television. Their expensive dress and sleek beauty identified them as a couple of Tupper Smith's call girls.

No one else was in the room, so I moved to a dining-room window. This room proved to be empty.

Rounding the corner of the house to the side porch, I moved silently to a kitchen window. The lace curtains here were drawn fully closed over the bottom pane, but were divided at the top. I dropped to my knees so that my head was just above the sill. The curtains were thick enough to prevent me from being seen in the outside darkness, yet thin enough so that I could see into the lighted room with relative clearness.

Three men and a delectable young woman with red hair sat around the kitchen table drinking beer. I recognized two of the men as Sheriff Merz and his deputy Gordy, the western-type clown I had twice before run into. The third I guessed must be Tupper Smith.

The owner of the farm was a lean, wire-hard man in his early forties with a thin, sharp-featured face and an arrogant expression. There was a quiet sort of cruelty in his face, a dangerous, chip-on-shoulder expression that marked him a man it wouldn't be wise to bluff. It was a face it would be a pleasure to bruise knuckles on.

As I watched, the peal of a phone bell sounded and the lean man rose to cross to a wall phone and lift the receiver. Because of the warm night, the lower part of the window I was looking through was open and had an insert screen in it. I could clearly hear the lean man say, "Hello," but the rest of his conversation was so low-toned, I couldn't make it out. He spoke more loudly after he hung up, however.

"There's a live one in room two-twenty of the Harrison Hotel," he said to the woman. "Want to take it?"

Sheriff Merz's husky voice objected, "I dropped over to see Doris particular, Tupper. I was just getting around to taking her upstairs. Send one of the gals out front."

The redheaded Doris didn't seem very enthusiastic about a liaison with the sheriff. Rising, she said, "Take one of the girls out front yourself, Sheriff. I'm not passing up a hundred and fifty bucks just to do you a favor."

The sheriff reached out, grasped her wrist and jerked her down into his lap. "Try to give me a brush-off and you'll be out of business altogether," he growled at her. She struggled, but he pinned her arms to her sides and held her forcibly against his chest.

The deputy Gordy watched this with a grin on his face, but Tupper Smith wasn't amused. He said in a flat voice, "Let her go!"

Merz glanced at the man in surprise. When he saw the pinched, flared-nostril expression on the farmer's face, he slowly released his grip on the redhead. She bounced from his lap, smoothed her skirt and gave the sheriff an angry look.

"I'll tell you what women you can or can't have," Smith said in the same flat voice. "I give the orders around here, and when I tell a girl to take a call, don't you ever tell her different."

Sheriff Merz had trouble deciding whether to take it or answer back. I could see his face redden as he stared at the lean farmer. Tupper Smith stared back, daring Merz to question his authority.

Finally Merz gave a crooked smile and shrugged. "Aw, hell," he said. "All chippies are alike in the dark anyway."

This ruffled the redhead. "What you think!" she flared at him.

The sheriff grinned at her, his good humor restored by her anger. Tupper Smith turned to the girl, dismissing the sheriff, and said, "You'll have to yell out the door for Matty, Doris. He's wandering around outside somewhere."

This was news to me. Unwelcome news. I had assumed that the light on the second floor meant the combination handyman-chauffeur Peggy had mentioned was up there.

But apparently he was outdoors with me. And the way my head must be silhouetted in the light from the window, I was lucky I didn't have a bullet through it.

The redheaded Doris headed for the kitchen door, which was right next to the window I crouched under. There wasn't time to make the front corner of the porch. On hands and kneees I scooted past the door, rose to my feet and vaulted the porch railing just as the door began to open.

I was around the corner, my back pressed against the rear of the house when her footsteps sounded on the porch.

"Matty!" she called. "Hey, Matty!"

When there was no response, she walked to the rear railing, leaned her hands on it and stared back toward the barn. She wasn't three feet from where I was flattened against the house, and if she had glanced down, she couldn't have avoided seeing me. Fortunately her attention was on the barn.

"Matty!" she called again. "Hey, Matty!"

A figure appeared at the rear corner of the barn and looked toward her. Apparently the man had been standing behind it enjoying the moonlit night. "Yeah?" he called.

As the moon was on the opposite side of the house, I stood in deep shadow. From his approximately hundred-foot distance I knew he couldn't see me, but if he walked directly toward the girl, he couldn't miss me. He would pass within two feet.

"Got a date in town!" Doris yelled. "Get out the car!"

"Okay," he yelled back.

He came along the edge of the barn and I thought he was going to walk straight at me. Instead he turned into the barn, obviously with the intention of driving the car parked in it out. The girl remained where she was, looking toward the barn.

It seemed apparent that Matty meant to back out and drive the car over alongside the side porch steps to pick up the girl, which meant his headlights would spear directly at me. I was afraid even a slight movement on my part would catch Doris's eye, but staying where I was meant certain detection. Slowly I edged farther along the rear of the house away from her.

After ten feet, with no sign from the girl that she had noticed my movement, I let out a silent sigh of relief. I was now far enough from her to make discovery unlikely even if she glanced my way, for compared to the moonlit yard, the shadow I was in was ebon black. I began to edge my way on, intending to step around the far corner when I reached it.

I had taken perhaps two more steps when I froze again. Matty came back out of the barn.

"Left the keys in the house," he called disgustedly, and headed for the back door.

He might have missed me anyway, since he was in bright moonlight and I was in shadow, if Fang hadn't picked that moment to reappear. The dog drifted into sight from no-where and fell in at Matty's side.

"Hello, mutt," Matty said to him.

I heard Doris's footsteps receding toward the side door, which was one problem off my mind, but I immediately acquired another. Fang spotted my motionless figure and came trotting over to me with his stub of a tail wagging. Matty by that time was beyond me nearly to the rear porch, and probably wouldn't have spotted me if he hadn't stopped to look back at the dog.

The screen door slammed, indicating Doris had gone back inside, at the same instant Matty said, "Hey! Who's that?"

There was less than ten feet between us. Instead of an-swering, I went toward him in a rush. He was a big, flat-faced man with huge shoulders and a chest as barrelled as Fang's, but his reactions were slow. I chopped a hard right into his jaw before he realized he was being swung at. It spun him around and dropped him to his knees with his back to me. It wasn't the time or the place for Marquis of Queensberry rules. I put him flat on his face with a rabbit punch behind the left ear.

Apparently Matty was a pal of Fang's because the dog didn't like this at all. A low growl swung me toward him, to find him crouching and showing all his teeth.

"Easy, Fang," I said in a soothing tone, backing away.

He wasn't having any. He stalked me on stiff legs, still snarling. Apparently he wasn't yet sure enough that I was an enemy to leap me, though. I backed clear to the far corner of the house without his doing anything except fol-low, stiff-legged, and growl. Perhaps I could have backed all the way up the lane to my car if the screen door hadn't slammed a second time just as I reached the corner.

Then Doris's voice screamed, "Tupper! Something's happened to Matty!"

The screen door slammed again and heavy feet sounded on the porch. I saw the lean farmer bend over the rear porch rail, look down at his prostrate handyman and then glance my way just as I backed around the corner.

"Get him, Fang!" Tupper Smith yelled. "After him, boy!"

Without hesitation the dog leaped at my throat.

chapter nineteen

THE REFLEX ACTION of throwing my left arm in front of my face was all that saved me from having my throat torn out. The huge jaws closed about my forearm, bringing me to my knees. I could feel teeth sink into the flesh through the cloth of my coat and shirt.

Fang stood spraddle-legged, his jaws gripping my arm like those of an English bulldog. He was all set to hold me there permanently, or at least until his master ordered him to let go.

I didn't co-operate very well. Raising my right fist, I crashed it down between his eyes with the force of a sledge hammer. The eyes crossed and he opened his jaws to stagger backward a pace.

Tupper Smith rounded the corner of the building at a run then, a snub-nosed revolver in his hand. I reached out and gripped Fang by both forelegs.

The dog must have weighed close to a hundred pounds, but you can handle a lot of weight when your veins are full of adrenalin. According to the medical books, it is fright that pumps adrenalin into your bloodstream. Mine must have been full of it, for the dazed dog seemed almost weightless when I scooped him up and slammed him into the running farmer's face.

They both went down in a confused tangle of man and animal just in time for the deputy Gordy to round the corner, trip over the tangle and fall flat on his face. I delayed long enough to dropkick the gun from Gordy's hand and see it arc off into the darkness. Then I turned and sprinted down the lane.

It was probably the fastest hundred-yard dash I ever made. It was too bad there was no official timer, because it may have been the fastest anyone ever made. I was urged on to break records by Sheriff Merz, who arrived at the corner just as I began to work up speed and pumped a couple of bullets after me.

Or maybe it was only one. Two whizzed past my right ear close enough for me to feel the heat of their passage, but it may have been the same bullet. Once passing me, once me passing it.

The sheriff gave up when I was halfway to the road, because there isn't much point in trying to hit a moving target with a pistol at better than fifty yards. I made the last fifty without his encouragement.

Peggy was under the wheel and had the engine running when I jerked open the car door and jumped in beside her. Shifting into drive, she gunned away from there like a thoroughbred racehorse leaving the gate.

"What happened?" she asked in a frightened voice. "What were those shots?"

"Sheriff Merz taking target practice," I panted. "With me as the target. Don't spare the horses. They may come after us in a car."

She pressed down on the accelerator until the speedometer needle touched eighty and stayed there. I leaned forward to examine my left forearm by the dashlight, and saw red oozing through the fang holes torn in the cloth.

Peggy took her eyes from the road long enough to glance downward, and almost put us in the ditch when she saw the blood. Her gaze jerked back to the highway when the car's right-hand wheels ran off on the shoulder; she wrestled with the steering wheel and managed to swerve us back on the concrete.

"You're shot!" she said in a shocked voice.

"Just bitten," I told her. "Fang mistook me for a bone. Pay attention to your driving."

She disobeyed me long enough to cast one more quick look at my arm, then fixed her eyes on the road and kept them there. I slipped off my suit coat, rolled up the shirt sleeve and examined the arm again. There were four punctures, two on top and two underneath my forearm. The ones underneath were deepest—they had been made by the dog's long fighting fangs.

I pulled out my handkerchief and bound it tightly over the wounds. The arm throbbed dully, but by the time we got back to town the bleeding had stopped. There had been no sign of pursuit all the way in, which wasn't surprising, since Peggy held to a steady eighty all the way. With our head start a pursuing car would have had to hit a hundred in order to catch us.

Peggy drove directly to her Mercer Street apartment. Parking in front, she said, "I have a first-aid kit in my bathroom, Mike. Or do you think you'd better see a doctor?"

"A little disinfectant and a bandage will fix me up," I said. "I think it bled enough to make infection unlikely."

I went inside with her and sat on the edge of the bathtub while she played nurse. It was pleasant to be fussed over by so lovely a woman in spite of the discomfort. First she poured peroxide directly into the wounds, which made me grit my teeth as it bubbled out again, presumably taking any lurking germs with it. Then she painted them with Mercurochrome and pasted a small Band-Aid over each puncture.

"I think I'll live," I said, rolling my shirt sleeve down and buttoning the cuff. "Thanks."

"You're welcome, Mike. What happened out there? Why did Fang jump you?"

"Tupper Smith ordered him to." I walked out into the front room and Peggy followed. "Got anything to drink around here? I'll tell you all about it over a nightcap."

She had some Old Granddad and some soda. I got a tray of ice from the refrigerator in the kitchen and mixed drinks while Peggy laid out dishes of peanuts and potato chips on the front-room cocktail table. Then we alternately munched and sipped while I described what had happened at the farm.

"It seems pretty evident that Sheriff Merz is hand in glove with Tupper Smith in the call-girl operation," I summed up. "If I could get a witness out there to overhear the same sort of conversation I overheard tonight, we'd have both Smith and the sheriff cold. It would be enough evidence to force the County District Attorney to take action."

"You're not going to risk another visit, are you?" Peggy asked in an appalled tone. "They'll be on guard now. Besides, you couldn't get past Fang."

"Yeah, there's that," I admitted reluctantly. "Though a hot dog with a little chloral hydrate injected into it might put Fang out of commission long enough to get my evidence. Will he take food from anyone but Smith?"

"I don't know," she said. "I've never heard Tupper mention it."

I swished the ice around in my glass and stared at it broodingly. "For Gloria's sake—Gladys', rather—I have to wind this case up fast. She's in constant danger until I do."

"Where do you have her hidden, Mike?"

I looked at her and shook my head. "I'm not telling anyone that, Peggy. I haven't even told my boss. I want her to stay alive."

Peggy flushed. "You don't think I'd turn her in to Tupper Smith, do you? Gladys is one of my best friends."

"I don't think anything," I said. "I'm just not taking chances with the girl's life."

"I'd like to see her, Mike," Peggy said in an earnest voice. "She must be half crazy with grief over Harry. Maybe I could cheer her up a bit. Or at least let her cry on my shoulder. I might even be able to arrange to get off work for a few days and stay with her. She shouldn't be all alone."

I started to open my mouth to say she wasn't all alone, then closed it again when I thought of my dissatisfaction with Alice Dill as a companion for Gladys. I would feel a lot easier with someone like Peggy Coynes at the river cottage instead of the flighty Alice.

Eyeing Peggy speculatively, I asked, "Think you could get off work?"

"I'm sure I can. Not tomorrow, because the store's expecting me in, and I couldn't reach my department head at this time of night. But I could pack a bag to take to work with me in the morning, and you could drive me to where Gladys is staying right after work."

I thought this over, and the more I thought about it, the better I liked the idea. "Okay," I decided. "I'll pick you up when the store closes and run you up to the cottage. We'll stop for dinner on the way."

"The cottage?" she asked.

"I have her hidden at the river cottage Harry owned. About thirty-five miles from town."

I drained my glass, waited till Peggy followed suit, picked

up both empty glasses and rose to go to the kitchen and make two more drinks. "This date was supposed to be a mixture of business and pleasure," I said. "But so far it's been all business. My business day just ended. It's time to start on the pleasure."

She didn't say anything, but she turned a rosy color as I carried the glasses to the kitchen. While mixing drinks I heard her rise and walk into the bedroom. I took my time with the mixing, but she still hadn't reappeared when I got back to the front room. I set down the two full glasses and lit a cigarette.

Five minutes passed before the bedroom door opened. Peggy had changed to slippers and a diaphanous blue negligee which clung so loosely to her figure that it didn't outline a single curve. It didn't have to. The light from the bedroom behind her shined right through the thin material, silhouetting her perfect figure as though she were naked.

She was, obviously, under the negligee.

Punching out my cigarette, I rose to my feet. A little inanely I said in a husky voice, "I mixed a couple of drinks."

She said nothing. She merely continued to stand just outside the door, with the light behind her, looking at me in a breathless, waiting manner.

"Who's thirsty anyway?" I asked, more of myself than her. I moved toward her and she moved toward me at the same time.

We met halfway.

chapter twenty

THE NEXT MORNING I phoned Peggy at work at about ten o'clock to find out if she had been able to wrangle a few days off. When she said that she had, I told her that I'd pick her up at the store's main entrance at five-thirty.

Just before noon Sid Trask called to tell me he had again heard from Alice Dill, and everything at the cottage was quiet.

I said, "Maybe you won't like this, Trask, but I'm taking a different girl out to stay with your sister tonight. A friend of hers named Peggy Coynes."

"Peggy Coynes?" he repeated in a suspicious tone. "I never heard Gladys mention that name."

I didn't think he'd take kindly to the information that the probable reason his sister had never mentioned her friend to him was that Peggy had been a fellow call girl. Instead I told him tactfully, "Nevertheless they're good friends. Peggy's a dress model at Stoyle's. Since your girl friend Alice seems to find life at the cottage so confining, I thought a relief companion for Gladys would be to everyone's advantage."

He mulled this over before asking, "You're sure this girl is all right? She won't go blabbing to anybody where Gladys is?"

I said bluntly, "She's probably twice as level-headed as your girl friend Alice. Alice seems like a nice girl, but you admitted yourself that she's bored with life at the cottage. I've been worried all along that she might do something silly like running into some congenial people in Clement and inviting them out to a party at the cottage."

He said, "Alice wouldn't do anything like that," but his tone was more defensive than assured.

"Well, at the very least she'll be glad to be relieved," I said. "I've already made arrangements to drive Peggy out tonight. She hasn't a car, so I thought I'd leave mine at the cottage and ride back to town with Alice."

He was silent for a few moments. Then he said, "All right, Macauley. I'll go along, but you'd better be sure of this girl. If anything goes haywire, I'll hold you responsible."

"I'll accept the responsibility," I said.

"What time you planning to drive out?"

I told him I was picking up Peggy after work at five-thirty and that we planned to stop for dinner en route, which should get us to the cottage about seven-thirty or eight.

"All right," he said. "Alice is supposed to phone me from Clement again at six. I'll tell her to expect you."

After I hung up, I thought about Sid Trask's tone when he had said, "If anything goes haywire, I'll hold you responsible." He hadn't meant it as an idle threat. There had been an implacableness in his voice that meant if anything happened to his sister, he wasn't going to stop to ask questions. He was coming straight after me with mayhem in mind.

At exactly five-thirty I drove into the customer's parking lot at Stoyle's Department Store. I had told Peggy I would wait for her at the main entrance, so I strolled over that way and leaned against the side of the building.

All along the street stores and office buildings were disgorging employees, a good percentage of them young women. They went past me in a steady stream, some hurrying to catch busses, or perhaps to meet cocktail dates, others meandering along in the relaxed state of letdown that stems from just having finished another day's work. It was now early July, and bright, colorful print dresses studded the street, giving the whole downtown section a gay, vacation-like look.

I, too, was in the relaxed mood of just having finished another day's work. The lazy summer weather, the moving crowd, mostly made up of pretty young women, put me into a youthful, pixyish frame of mind. Lounging against the side of the building, I suddenly found myself engaging in a sport I hadn't played at since I was a teen-ager: ogling the legs of passing females.

I was giving the limbs of a shapely brunette who had just passed a particularly interested examination from the rear when an icy voice said at my shoulder, "Maybe she'll turn around if you whistle."

I think it's a tribute to my iron self-control that I didn't even give a guilty start. Unhurriedly turning to look down at Peggy Coynes' frown, I said gallantly, "I've been comparing passing female legs with yours. There isn't a pair in town that comes anywhere close."

She gave a disdainful sniff. "If I'd been five minutes more, you probably wouldn't have waited. From the lecherous expression on your face, you were plannning to whistle something down at any minute."

I've learned that the best defense against this sort of feminine accusation is total silence. Giving her a fond smile, I lifted the overnight bag she was carrying from her hand, took her elbow and steered her toward the parking lot. I wasn't the only man in town whom the warm weather had made conscious of feminine anatomy, I noticed. Every

male we passed, of any age, flashed Peggy a quick, apprecia-
tive look.

She deserved it. She was as fresh and starched-looking
in her bright cotton print dress as though she hadn't worked
a minute all day in the eighty-five-degree temperature we
had at the moment.

Peggy's natural disposition was too sunny for her to hold
a grudge very long. By the time we had driven a block, she
had forgotten my mental infidelity and was chattering as
gaily as usual. She wanted to know where we were going
to have dinner, and I told we'd stop near Titusgrove.

We stopped just short of Titusgrove at the same roadhouse where Sid Trask, his sister, Alice Dill and I had
dined the evening we hid Gladys out at the river cottage.
After a couple of martinis we had some delicious broiled
lobster. When we went on an hour later, we were both in
the mellow, relaxed, well-fed mood that comes only from
excellent food properly prepared.

It was just short of eight P.M. when we reached the dirt
road leading off the highway to the river cottage, and because of daylight saving time, it was still bright daylight.
As we turned off on the dirt road, I noticed an empty black
sedan parked on the highway shoulder a few yards beyond
the entrance.

As there was nothing to see along here but the river, I
idly wondered if some fisherman had parked the sedan there
and then walked the couple of hundred yards to the river.
If he had, I hoped it hadn't given the girls a scare to see a
strange man wandering around.

It never occurred to me to put any more sinister meaning
to the sedan. With the perfect weather, an excellent meal
inside of me and a lovely girl at my side, I was too full of
euphoria for any unpleasant thoughts to intrude.

I experienced a minor letdown to my feeling of well-
being when we got within sight of the cottage, though.
Alice Dill's yellow convertible wasn't in the car port beneath the building. Sid Trask had said she was going to
phone him from Clement at six P.M. Now it was nearly eight,
and Clement was only four miles off. It didn't take two
hours to drive four miles. Probably Alice had forgotten the
time and was sitting in some barroom in Clement.

Even though this thought mildly irked me, it also made

me glad of one thing: that I had decided to replace the un-reliable Alice Dill with Peggy Coynes.

I pulled into the car port, cut the ignition and said, "Well, we're at your new temporary home, Peggy."

Both of us climbed from the car. Peggy looked at the wooden stairs leading upward curiously.

"All the river cottages along here are built a full story off the ground," I explained. "Otherwise you'd have your living room under water during the spring floods."

Walking to the open back end of the car port, I shaded my eyes toward the river to see if perhaps Gladys was having an early-evening swim. There was no one in sight along the clay-and-gravel strip of beach.

"She's upstairs, I guess," I said to Peggy. "After you."

I motioned for her to precede me up the stairs, but she hung back. "You'd better go first, Mike," she said. "Gladys will be expecting you, but not me. I might frighten her."

Shrugging, I climbed the steps ahead of her. At the top I knocked, got no answer and, after a moment of waiting, tried the doorknob. The door was unlocked.

Standing in the open doorway, I called, "Gladys!"

There was dead silence. I stood there a moment more, conscious of Peggy patiently waiting on the step just behind me. Then, abruptly, the euphoria brought on by the warm weather, a too-substantial meal and a beautiful companion drained away. I tried to tell myself that Gladys was in one of the bedrooms asleep, and simply hadn't heard my call. But I couldn't convince myself of it.

Belatedly I was acutely aware of danger. The absence of Alice Dill's convertible suddenly took on a more sinister meaning than mere irresponsibility on her part. The empty black sedan parked just past the entrance to the dirt road all at once started ringing alarm bells in my head too.

Coming unfrozen, I stepped into the combination living room and kitchen. I heard Peggy's footstep on the top step behind me. Then a half-seen movement from the corner of my eye, or perhaps only a premonition of what was coming, caused me to drop face forward. It happened too suddenly for me to be sure just which brought on my instinctive reaction.

I wasn't quite fast enough. I was halfway to the floor, intending to fall flat and roll, when something heavy smashed into the back of my head. My second-last thought was a mixture of self-reproach for so easily walking into a trap, and overwhelming anger at Peggy.

My last thought was to wonder vaguely what she had hit me with.

chapter twenty-one

I DON'T BELIEVE I WAS OUT more than an hour. When I slowly came to, it was dark in the room where I found myself, but through a window facing me I could see that there was still a faint cast of light outdoors. Which meant it must be somewhere around nine.

For the moment I didn't do much thinking beyond that, because the back of my head was throbbing too hard. Vaguely I was aware that I was lying on a bed, and I remembered that last conscious instant after Peggy, or someone, had smashed me over the head from behind.

Then I was sidetracked from this remembrance by gradual awareness that something more than a mere bump on the head was wrong with me. The bed seemed to be rolling, as though I were on a ship riding a heavy sea. Dropping my feet over the side of the bed, I sat erect, letting out a deep groan when the movement drove a spike of pain into my skull.

Eventually the pain subsided to a dull ache, but the sensation of being on shipboard persisted. Standing up, I staggered across the room and prevented myself from falling only by grabbing the door jamb with both hands.

What was wrong with me penetrated then. I was about half drunk.

I stood there holding onto the door jamb with my eyes squeezed shut, trying to figure this out. Peggy and I had had two martinis apiece at the roadhouse, then topped them with a pair of two-and-a-half-pound lobsters soaked in butter. I knew I hadn't been even faintly tipsy when I walked into the cottage.

The smell of raw bourbon hit me then, and I had the answer. Enough had been forced down my throat while I was unconscious to give me the staggers. More had been poured over my clothing, or perhaps merely spilled in trying to make me swallow.

Gradually I oriented myself and realized I was standing in the doorway to one of the cottage's bedrooms. I staggered out into the combination living room-kitchen, caromed off the table and finally reached the sink. By now it was so dark that I had to grope for the handle of the pump over the sink.

Weakly I moved the handle up and down, after an eon being rewarded by the sound of a small trickle of water falling into the sink. This encouraged me to pump harder, and the flow of water quickly increased. When it was gushing with the force of a fire hydrant, I ducked my head under it, held it there and continued to pump.

I stopped pumping just short of drowning myself, turned my head sidewise and drank deeply from the diminishing flow. It was underground spring water, ice cold and as bracing as a full night's sleep.

I was nearly sober when I took my head out of the sink.

The next necessity was light. I found my cigarette lighter in my pocket, flicked it on and held it aloft. One of the Coleman lanterns with which the cottage was furnished sat on the kitchen table. I shook it, found it half full of gasoline and pumped in air. I snapped my lighter off before picking up the lantern, so I did this in the dark, all the time feeling water from my wet hair running down inside my collar.

Now I had to have a match, as I couldn't start the lamp with a lighter. By the lighter flame I discovered a box on a shelf over the stove. I lit one, stuck it through the ignition hole in the side of the lantern and fed gas. There was a hissing noise, a flickering blue flame licked over the twin mantles, then they glowed to the blinding brightness of a two-hundred-watt bulb.

Glancing around the room, I was mildly surprised to find it as disordered as it was. One of the kitchen chairs lay on its side on the floor near the sink. It was a miracle that I hadn't tripped headlong over it in the dark. Two open bottles of whisky stood on the sink drainboard, one nearly empty and the other half full. The lid of the ice compartment of the icebox stood open, and an icepick was buried in a melting chunk of ice. A large bowl of nearly melted ice on the drainboard suggested why the lid was open.

A couple of empty soda bottles had been carelessly dropped on the floor. Another, half full, stood on the table. Two glasses containing the dregs of highballs sat on the table too, an ash tray full of cigarettes between them. One of the glasses had lipstick on its rim. About half of the cigarette butts were also lipstick-stained. The other half, unstained, I noticed were the same brand I smoked.

The place had all the earmarks of having witnessed a drunken orgy.

Lifting the Coleman lantern by its handle, I carried it into one of the bedrooms. Not the one I had awakened in, for I had a strange reluctance to go back in there. The bed in this room was made up and there were no clothes in either the closet or the dresser drawers. I wondered which of the two women's rooms it had been.

The only room left to inspect was the bedroom where I had awakened. Bracing myself, I carried the gasoline lantern in there.

Here, too, were signs of the same drunken orgy that apparently had started in the combination living room and kitchen. A three-quarters-empty bottle of whisky stood on the floor alongside the bed, an empty soda bottle lay on its side in one corner and two empty glasses kept company with another full ash tray on the bedside stand. Again one of the glasses was lipstick-stained, as were half of the cigarette butts.

One of the participants in the apparent orgy was still there too. She lay on her back on the wall side of the same bed I had been lying on. It was Gladys Allerup, nee Gladys Trask, alias Gloria Townsend. She was stark naked and she was all through with partying.

She had been strangled to death.

It didn't take a deductive genius to figure out what was *supposed* to have happened in the cottage. All the clues indicated that the dead woman and some man had thrown a super-dooper of a duet party which ended in a drunken attack and murder by the man. I didn't have to strain my mental powers beyond their limit to decide that since my brand of cigarettes was mixed with Gladys' in the two ash trays, undoubtedly my fingerprints were all over the whisky and soda bottles and on the glasses which lacked lipstick stains.

The only thing that puzzled me was why the police hadn't arrived before I woke up.

There was nothing I could do for Gladys. This time, unlike the occasion at the Lagoon, there was no doubt that she was dead. I carried the lantern out into the main room again, then down the wooden stairs to the car port beneath the cottage. There was no sign of my car.

Walking out from beneath the car port, I held the lantern high. Its bright glow lighted the area for a hundred-foot radius. Nothing but trees and underbrush was in sight.

It was a four-mile walk to the nearest town, Clement, and I didn't feel up to it at the moment. I went back upstairs, lit a cigarette and sat at the kitchen table to figure things out.

It seemed probable for a number of reasons that Peggy Coynes had played me for a patsy. Trusting her, I had told her where Gladys was, and she had had a whole day to transmit the information to Tupper Smith before I picked her up after work. It didn't seem likely that the information could have leaked from anyone else, because Sid Trask and Alice Dill were the only two other people aside from me who knew where Gladys was hidden out. Sid certainly wouldn't have leaked it, and I could see no motive for his girl friend to turn traitor. That left Peggy.

I wondered what the killer, or killers, had done with Alice Dill. Her car being missing suggested that at best she had been kidnapped. Or more probably murdered. I didn't like to think of what plans Sid Trask would have for me if both his sister and girl friend were dead.

I wrenched my thoughts back to Peggy Coynes, still not wanting to believe she was nothing but a spy for the call-girl gang. If she had been planted by Tupper Smith to work on me and find out where Gladys was hidden, she was the most expert actress I ever ran across. I would have sworn she was sincere in her claim that she wanted to get out of the call-girl racket, and in her fear of Tupper Smith.

Maybe that was the answer, I told myself, wanting to find some justification for her. Maybe she was so terrified of the lean farmer, she was willing to do anything to pacify him.

Peggy had been right behind me when I was hit over the head, and my last thought had been to wonder what she had hit me with. I had a vague recollection of seeing another movement, possibly that of someone hiding behind the door, but I wasn't sure of it. And if Peggy hadn't been part of the plot, why wasn't she as dead as Gladys? If she hadn't been my assailant, obviously she saw who was, and the killer wouldn't have left her alive.

There was no sign that anything violent had happened to her. It seemed evident that she had driven off in my car under her own power.

Which meant she had to be part of the plot.

Punching out my cigarette, I leaned toward the highball glass on the table which lacked lipstick stains and blew my breath on it. When it misted over, five fingerprints appeared. They were so carefully placed, there wasn't any doubt in my mind that they were mine, and that they had been pressed there while I was unconscious. With normal handling there would have been numerous prints overlapping each other, most of them smudged.

I got out my handkerchief and wiped the glass clean. Then I wiped the lipstickless glass in the bedroom and every bottle in the place, including the empty ones.

I wasn't worried about destroying evidence, because I knew it was all planted evidence.

When I had finished this, I covered my hand with the handkerchief and put all the whisky bottles away in the cupboard. The empty soda bottles I lined up neatly under the sink. There was a garbage can under the sink and I emptied both ash trays into it. When I had picked up the overturned chair, dumped the ice bowl into the sink and closed the lid of the ice compartment, there was no sign of a drinking party having taken place in the cottage.

I had just finished when I heard the whine of an approaching siren on the highway. The sound swelled nearer and nearer, then abruptly droned off into silence.

Apparently the driver had cut it when he turned off the highway onto the dirt road, for a few moments later headlights flashed on the kitchen windows. I walked over to one of the windows to look out, and saw that I had official visitors.

A car with flashing red lights on top was parked just beyond the car port, and a man was climbing from either side of it.

chapter twenty-two

I HAD ONE FINAL THING TO DO before I was ready to face law officers. Pulling a dish towel from a rack by the sink, I rubbed my wet hair as dry as I could get it, then hurriedly ran my pocket comb through it. There was nothing I could do about my wet shirt collar, but it was a hot night, and possibly the dampness would pass for perspiration.

Footsteps sounded on the wooden stairs. I didn't wait for a knock and a demand for entry. I opened the door and said to the fat deputy sheriff who was three-quarters of the way up, "It sure took you long enough."

Apparently he wasn't expecting to find anyone alive in the cottage. He stopped short, his hand flashing toward his pistol holster. Then my words registered on him, he slowly released the gun butt and started up again.

He was a plump, large-eared man in his fifties with a round face that looked stupid at first glance. Shrewd little eyes gave him away, though. He was one of those cops who make a point of looking stupid in order to throw suspects off guard.

The man who followed him up the steps was younger, somewhere in his mid-twenties. He was tall, handsome and dumb-looking. Only with him it wasn't an act. Both were dressed in blue shirts, white riding breeches and boots, and wore white Stetsons.

When they were both inside, the plump deputy looked me up and down and inquired mildly, "Who are you, Bub?"

I pulled out my wallet and let him have a look at the card behind the plastic shield. He studied it silently, then looked at me again and waited. He was going to let me make the next move.

Stuffing my wallet back in my pocket, I said briskly, "The body's in here." I lifted the Coleman lantern from the table and led the way into Gladys's bedroom.

Both men stood looking at the corpse for a time without saying anything. Then the younger one went over, lifted

97

one of the dead woman's wrists and felt for pulse, verifying my opinion that his dumb look was no act. The girl's face was a light blue color, her swollen tongue protruded from her open mouth, and her eyes bulged half out of her head. Even from clear across the room it was obvious that she'd been strangled and had been dead for some time.

He said, "Yeah, she's gone all right, Mort."

His plump partner didn't answer. Instead he walked back into the main room, hitched his rump onto a corner of the table and looked me up and down again. His eyes centered on my wet collar and seemed to be examining it appraisingly.

I was just beginning to feel uneasy under the examination when he stuck a forefinger under his own collar and pulled it away from his throat to let in air. Then I saw that his collar, and his whole shirt for that matter, was as damp as mine. My wetness had only reminded him of the heat.

"Maybe you'd like to tell me about it," he suggested.

"Mind introducing yourselves first?" I inquired. "I don't want to have to call you Bub, or Hey, You."

He looked at me expressionlessly for a minute. Then he said, "I'm Mort Gerard. My partner's Frank Wesson. We're both deputy sheriffs of Black County."

I turned to young Frank Wesson, who hadn't seen my identification card when I showed it to Gerard. "I'm Mike Macauley," I said. "With the D.A.'s office in the city."

Wesson looked puzzled. "What you doing out here then? You got no jurisdiction in Black County."

His plump partner said, "That's what I been wondering, mister."

"The dead woman is a Miss Gladys Trask," I told him. I paused. "Mrs. Gladys Allerup, rather. She was just recently married. She was a material witness in the gang murder of her husband a few days back. A cop named Harry Allerup. Maybe you read about it in the papers."

Mort Gerard nodded. "I read about it."

"My office believed she was in danger of being murdered by the same people who killed her husband. With good reason, obviously. I've had her hidden out here until I could collect enough evidence to take to court."

"Alone?" the plump man asked.

I shook my head. "With a friend named Alice Dill. What's happened to her, I don't know. Neither she nor her car were here when I arrived a while back. She's probably been either kidnapped or murdered."

Gerard asked casually, "How long ago is a while back?"

I glanced at my watch and saw it was nine-thirty. "I'm not sure," I said. "Finding my star witness dead upset me too much to think of looking at the time. An hour, maybe. It was still light." I thought it was reasonably safe to cut a half hour from the time I'd been at the cottage. If it ever came out that I'd arrived before eight, I could claim I'd simply underestimated the passage of time.

When Gerard studied me with his shrewd little eyes, I decided putting him on the defensive would be the best method of sidetracking whatever suspicions he might be harboring about me. "What took you so long getting here?" I asked.

He wasn't easy to sidetrack. "How did you know we was coming?" he countered.

"Because as soon as I discovered the body, I sent my companion into town to phone the sheriff's office," I said testily. "You don't see any car parked outside, do you? How do you think I got here?"

He shook his head slowly. "You tell me."

"A friend and I drove out in my car. When I found my witness dead, I sent my companion to find a phone and call you. There's no phone here, you know. I stayed to wait for somebody from the sheriff's office to show."

His suspicion seemed to lessen a little, but he still wasn't ready to swallow my story whole. "What was your friend's name?" he asked.

I began to sweat a little. I had deliberately kept the sex of my "companion" vague, because I didn't know whether a man or a woman had phoned in an anonymous report. I only knew that someone had, because otherwise the two deputies wouldn't be here.

I bluffed it out by asking with faint but obvious disapproval, "For cripes sake, didn't your desk man ask?"

"Sure," he said. "But she wouldn't say. Just said somebody was hurt, or maybe dead, out here, described how to get here and hung up."

I breathed a silent sigh of relief. The caller had been a woman.

"She's a girl named Peggy Coynes," I said. "If you want to question her as a witness, her home address is Apartment B, three twenty-four Mercer, and she works in the dress department at Stoyle's Department Store."

That should do it, I thought. If Peggy was ever picked up, she'd either have to go along with my story or implicate herself. No one in on the frame would be able to mention the evidence of the drinking party I was supposed to have thrown with Gladys, unless he was also willing to answer embarrassing questions as to how he knew about the evidence.

The young deputy pulled out a notebook and wrote down the information I had just given. Mort Gerard allowed his eyebrows to climb. "Ain't she coming back here?"

"No," I said. "I told her to drive back to town and break the news of his sister's death to the dead woman's brother. I figured I could ride into Titusgrove with you and catch a taxi from there."

The plump man's eyebrows went up even more. "You sent off a witness to a murder before she could talk to the police?"

"She's no witness," I told him. "She didn't even come in. She waited in the car while I came in to see Mrs. Allerup. All she could tell you was that I sent her off to phone the sheriff's office."

He pushed back his Stetson and rubbed the back of one hand over a bald brow, thinking. Eventually he said, "I guess I believe you, Macauley. Can't think why a guy from the D.A.'s office would want to knock off a material witness. But just to be safe, I think I'll phone your boss when we get back to the office. Sunshine Sever's still the D.A. down there, ain't he?"

"Yeah," I said. "That suits me fine. I want to report this to him anyway."

His next words told me that he had finally decided to accept me at face value, and was prepared to offer the courtesy of one law enforcement official to another. "We'll try to get your part of this thing wound up as soon as possible, but there'll be a few more questions we'll want the answers to down at the office before I can let you go. Who your suspects are in this gang that bumped Mrs. Allerup's husband, for instance, and what you think their motive was."

"Of course," I said. "With the first murder in our jurisdiction and the second in yours, both offices will have to co-operate."

"One thing I don't understand, though," he said. "Why'd this Coynes woman refuse to give her name when she called in?"

I shrugged. "Maybe she was upset. Or maybe she thought she'd be held up for questioning and wanted to get back to town in a hurry to break the news to Mrs. Allerup's brother. She's a pretty good friend of the family. Women do crazy things under stress."

"Yeah," he said a little glumly. "I'm married to one." He slid his rump from the table. "Well, let's go. I got to call the state police lab and have them go over this place. Plus get the coroner out here. You didn't touch anything, did you?"

"The body's exactly as I found it," I said truthfully.

chapter twenty-three

THE BLACK COUNTY Sheriff's Office was in Titusgrove. All the way during the drive in I kept thinking of what Sid Trask's reaction was going to be when he heard what had happened. With his sister dead and his girl friend missing, I was afraid I was going to have a maniac on my hands.

At that time of night the sheriff himself wasn't on duty. Mort Gerard took advantage of this by making use of the sheriff's private office instead of using the phone in the squadroom. I sat waiting in a leather-backed chair while he got out an all-points bulletin on the missing Alice Dill, then phoned the state police lab and the county coroner to set both in motion.

When he had finished this business, he turned to me. "Know where I can reach Sever at this time of night, Macauley?"

I gave him Sunshine's home phone number and he dialed long distance. A few moments later he said into the mouthpiece, "Mr. Sever? This is Black County Deputy Sheriff Gerard calling from Titusgrove. We got a murder up here, and our chief witness is an assistant of yours named Macauley."

He listened for a moment, then began to describe the circumstances of the murder and my role as a witness.

When he finished, he looked at me. "Your boss wants to talk to you, Macauley."

I rose, took the receiver and said, "Hi, Sunshine."

He was having mild apoplexy. "What in the seven levels of hell are you going to do next, Mike?" he inquired. "Now you've gone and gotten our only witness to the Allerup kill bumped off. And not even in our own jurisdiction."

I said coldly, "What do you mean, I got her bumped off?"

"It was you who hid her out, wasn't it? Why didn't you put her in jail for protection? It's legal to hold a material witness in jail, you know, in case you missed the day they taught that in law school."

"Jail wouldn't have been any safer then the cottage," I said bitterly, ignoring his heavy sarcasm. "In case *you* didn't know it, there's at least one influential official right in town tied in with the call-girl racket."

He was silent for a minute. Then he asked in a different tone, "Where'd you get that information?"

"From Allerup's wife. He told her before he was killed." I waited, and when he didn't say anything more, asked, "Did you vouch for me to Deputy Gerard, or tell him to toss me in the clink as a suspicious character?"

"I told him you were at the cottage on authorized official business," he said wearily. "See you in the morning. Early. Drop into my office as soon as you get there."

Another session on the carpet, I thought as I hung up. This whole case had brought me nothing but grief. Half the time I was banging my head against the stone wall of official red tape, the other half I was on the carpet in Sunshine Sever's office.

Mort Gerard motioned me back to my seat and began asking questions. He wanted to know the background on the Harry Allerup murder. If the killing had taken place in Sheriff Merz's jurisdiction, I wouldn't have volunteered the time of day. But Black County was run on a different basis than Merz ran his territory, and there wasn't any point in not giving full co-operation.

I told him the whole background of the call-girl investigation, including the unpublicized fact that Allerup had been a crooked cop and a member of the gang. I even threw in a description of my visit to Tupper Smith's farm, and told him of my belief that Sheriff Merz was accepting a pay-off to protect the racket.

"A good deal of this is off the record, of course," I finished up. "We don't want any mention of Allerup's connection with the gang to leak to the papers, because we don't want Smith and his cronies to know that we're aware of the motive for his murder. And Sheriff Merz would probably sue for defamation of character if you passed on what I've told you about him."

"Yeah," he said. "I guess the best bet is just to play it as a mysterious murder, far as the papers are concerned." He frowned. "If Merz is protecting this Tupper Smith, how we ever going to pin either kill on the gang? Not much point in asking Sheriff Merz for co-operation. And we can't go down in his county to pull in Smith for questioning without going through Merz."

I gave him a sour grin. "Now you're beginning to see the problem I've been up against since I was first handed this call-girl thing. A little frustrating, isn't it?"

He gave a disgusted grunt.

By now we were getting along so chummily, I decided to stretch my luck. Still thinking of Sid Trask's probable reaction, I said, "Can I ask you a favor, Gerard?"

"Sure," he said. "What's up?"

"Can you keep the lid on Mrs. Allerup's murder for twenty-four hours?"

He frowned at me. "Not give it to the papers, you mean? Reporters get pretty touchy about that."

"I need a little time to pull together some loose ends," I explained. "It's going to be a lot easier for me if the story doesn't break immediately."

He scratched his bald brow and pulled at one of his oversized ears as he thought this over. Finally he said in a reluctant voice, "We want to co-operate with your office in any reasonable way. Suppose I hold it till the final edition tomorrow evening. That way the news will hit the streets about nine P.M."

This was almost as good as twenty-four hours. At least it would give me all day tomorrow to attempt to crack the case and hand Sid Trask the answer when he came gunning for me.

We parted on cordial terms a few minutes later, each of us promising to keep the other informed of any developments. Gerard called me a taxi from the sheriff's office, and I got back to my Wren Street apartment about eleven-thirty.

I got a surprise when I climbed out of the cab. My car was parked in front of the apartment building.

When the taxi drove off, I went over to the car and looked inside. The keys were in the ignition. Dropping them in my pocket, I went upstairs and checked my flat. No one was there, and there was no sign that anyone had been.

I checked the phone book for Peggy Coyne's number and dialed her apartment. When there was no answer after twelve rings, I hung up and dialed Homicide. I got Sergeant Johnny Sullivan on the phone.

"Mike Macauley, Johnny," I told him. "I suppose you got the all-points bulletin on Alice Dill."

"Yeah, just a while ago," he said in a surprised voice. "How'd you know about it? It came from Titusgrove."

I didn't want to break the news to him just then that our only witness in the Allerup case was dead. I had heard enough reproaches from Sunshine Sever to last me for one night. I said, "Tell you about it when I see you. Meantime could you do me a favor?"

"Sure, Mike. What you need?"

"I want another pickup order put out. Just a local, not an all-points, and I want you to keep it under your hat. Just a quiet covering of the airport, railroad station, bus depot and so on."

"I get you. Who's the suspect and what's the charge?"

"Her name's Peggy Coynes, alias Penny Coynes. She's a slim, delicate-featured blonde about twenty-five years old. Five three or four, about a hundred and ten pounds. Exceptionally good-looking and exceptionally shapely. At first glance she looks like a teen-ager."

"Hmm," Sullivan said. "I may go out on this personally. What did you say the charge was?"

I started to say, "Material witness in a murder case," then realized I'd have to tell him who was murdered. As the murder had occurred in Black County, it wasn't any of Sullivan's official business, and I didn't want to go through all the necessary explanation. I said, "Make up a charge. And let me know the minute you net her, no matter what time it is. I'll come right down to talk to her."

"Hmm," he said again. "You're not using police facilities to track down some gal for romantic reasons, are you?"

"Don't be silly," I told him. "This is official business."

He laughed. "Wouldn't put it past you. Okay, Mike. Will do."

After I hung up I realized I still had a throbbing headache from the blow I had taken, though it seemed to be improving by the minute. I decided to speed recovery a little. A hot shower followed by an ice cold one was the first part of the therapy. Two aspirin and a cold highball in a tall glass was the second part.

I sat in the front room in my pajamas, sipping my nightcap and mulling over the events of the evening before I went to bed. All-in-all it added up to about the worst evening I had ever spent. The murder of my only witness in the Allerup case, plus Peggy Coynes' treachery, brought the call-girl investigation to a fresh standstill. With neither girl available to testify, I couldn't even stick Tupper Smith on a procuring charge, let alone drag him into court for murder.

The worst thing of all, though, was having to face the fact that my judgement of Peggy could have been so wrong. I still didn't want to face it, and in the back of my mind there was yet a faint hope that I had somehow misinterpreted her part in the evening's events.

I realized this was the subconscious reason I had put out a quiet pickup order on her instead of the routine all-points bulletin I would have requested for any other material witness. I wanted to talk to her personally and hear from her own lips what explanation she had, if any, before throwing her to the official wolves.

chapter twenty-four

As soon as I got to the office the next morning I called the sheriff's office at Titusgrove. Mort Gerard wasn't on duty days, but another deputy told me that no report on Alice Dill had as yet come in. He said the state police lab's report was mainly negative too. A half dozen sets of prints had been lifted in the cottage, but so far none except the dead woman's had been identified. The coroner's report said that Gladys Allerup had died of manual strangulation, and fixed the time of death as between seven-thirty and eight-thirty P.M.

He had one other bit of information that puzzled me. My "companion" had phoned an anonymous tip about the murder to the state police as well as to the sheriff's office, and they had arrived at the cottage shortly after the two deputies and I left.

After talking to Titusgrove I went into Sunshine Sever's office to get that ordeal over with. The D.A. was seated behind his desk with his coat off and his collar open at the throat, all two hundred and fifty pounds of him already suffering from the heat, although it was only about seventy-five at that time of morning. I felt sorry for him, because the weather man predicted ninety by noon.

He didn't even say good morning. He opened the conversation by saying, "Mike, this is a hell of a mess."

I took a chair next to his desk, lit a cigarette and said, "Yeah."

"Wait till the commissioner hears what happened. He'll go right through the roof. He'll want to know why we didn't request police protection for Mrs. Allerup."

I said, "Tell him because somebody with power enough to pull strings in his police department is heading up the call-girl racket. Maybe the commissioner himself."

Sunshine looked startled. "Are you out of your mind? Harry Allerup didn't tell his wife *that*, did he?"

"He referred to a 'big boss.' And he didn't mean Tupper Smith or Sheriff Merz. Smith is just the front for the operation, and I know he doesn't take orders from Merz. As a matter of fact it's *vice versa*."

The D.A. raised his eyebrows. "How do you know that?"

I told him about my visit to Tupper Smith's farm, and the minor clash I had witnessed between Smith and the sheriff over the redheaded Doris.

He shook his head wearily when I finished. "Mike, I told you to stay out of Merz's territory. It would look fine in the papers if you'd been arrested for trespassing."

I felt like laughing in his face. I had barely gotten away with my life after being mauled by a dog and then shot at, and Sunshine was worried about a trespassing charge.

Sunshine said, "Aside from the hearsay statement of a dead woman, what evidence do you have that someone in the city heads the call-girl racket?"

"No actual evidence," I admitted. "But lots of indications. Somebody with power has been throwing official roadblocks in my way ever since I started poking into the call-girl racket. Look at the way I was kept from questioning Harry Allerup, for instance. That was deliberate, Sunshine."

He mopped a dripping forehead with an oversized handkerchief. "It could have been coincidence, Mike. You haven't any proof it wasn't."

"Maybe I will have," I told him. "I asked Stan Spooner to make discreet inquiries as to who suggested Allerup for that Chicago trip. Mark Towner, the chief of detectives, was the one who actually sent him, but I'm betting his name was suggested by the man Allerup called the 'big boss.' I'm going to check with Spooner today to find out if he learned anything."

The district attorney slowly shook his head. "No you're not, Mike. I'll check with him myself."

I hiked a couple of eyebrows. "What's that crack supposed to mean?

"It means I'm pulling you off the call-girl investigation. You've stirred too many people up and made too many mistakes. Letting a material witness in your custody get killed was the last straw. I'm going to have a lot of explaining to do when I talk to the commissioner. He's going to want the blame fixed somewhere, and you're where it belongs. I'm going to tell him I've pulled you off and have taken over personally.'"

I stared at him for a while, then got up without saying anything, ground out my cigarette in his desk ash tray and walked out the door. I could see him bracing himself for the door to slam, so I closed it quietly.

At any previous time up to that moment I would have been glad to be relieved of the call-girl investigation. But not now—not after having a witness murdered right under my nose and then having the killer try to frame me for the murder. It was now more than a mere official duty. It was a personal fight between me and the operators of the racket, and I had no intention of quitting, orders or no orders, until the ring was smashed.

I stayed in my office only long enough to glance over my mail, then told Miss Rains I was going over to Police Headquarters.

I dropped by Homicide first, where I found that Johnny

Sullivan had left me a message to the effect that Peggy Coynes hadn't as yet been located, but the search was going on. I knew that meant he not only was having the various transportation outlets covered, but was having police make a systematic check of hotels. If Peggy was still in town, eventually Johnny Sullivan would find her.

From Homicide I went over to the Morals Division office, where I found Lieutenant Stan Spooner as usual up to his neck in paper work. He pushed it aside when I came in, gave me a reserved smile and said, "Morning, Mike."

"How are you, Stan?" I asked. I took a seat and lit a cigarette. "Had a chance to talk to Captain Towner yet?"

"About Harry Allerup? Yes, I dropped a couple of casual questions." He gave me a peculiar look. "I don't quite understand why you asked me to sound him out, Mike."

I looked at him blankly. "I told you the other day. I thought learning who brought pressure to have Allerup sent to Chicago might lead me to the local head of the call-girl racket."

He nodded slowly. "Yes, I know what you told me. But you must have known."

"I must have known what?"

"That the suggestion to send Allerup on detached service came from you."

I let my mouth hang open. "From me!"

"Well, from the district attorney's office. Towner didn't say from who over there, and I didn't ask him because I didn't want him to know I was pumping him. You said to keep it discreet."

I absorbed this in stunned silence. No wonder Sunshine Sever had pulled me off the investigation the instant I mentioned I had asked Lieutenant Spooner to do a little under-cover work. The reason he had given—that the police commissioner would insist on someone taking the blame for Gladys Allerup's death—had been pure cover-up. He simply hadn't wanted me to learn that he himself was the official who had been pulling strings to stymie my efforts.

I butted my cigarette and rose. "Thanks, Stan," I said. "You've been a big help. A bigger help than you know."

chapter twenty-five

BACK AT THE OFFFICE again I sat at my desk for a long time, brooding. I could still hardly believe that Sunshine Sever was the head of the call-girl racket. He was a politician through and through, but I had always considered him a reasonably honest politician.

I was losing a lot of illusions lately. First the girl I had trusted and liked—had almost more than liked—had deliberately played me for a patsy, to all appearances. Now my own boss, whom I had also trusted and liked, if not exactly respected, seemed to have played me for a sucker too.

The worst of it was that I still had no real evidence. I was gaining more knowledge of the call-girl setup by the day, but I didn't have a single item I could take before a grand jury. I could imagine the jury foreman asking, "What proof do you have, Mr. Macauley, that the District Attorney heads this alleged call-girl racket?" and my answering, "Well, he suggested to the chief of detectives that a Morals Division sergeant named Harry Allerup be sent on detached service to Chicago once."

The thought was too silly to carry further. I had to get real evidence somewhere, somehow.

My one hope was that Peggy Coynes would be found, for she was the sole witness I had who could tell a grand jury anything at all about the call-girl setup. All I could do was wait for Sullivan to find her.

At noon Sid Trask phoned, but I told Miss Rains to say I wasn't in. There was no point in talking to him. Time was running short and I couldn't afford to be sidetracked by having to duck bullets from Trask. If I had talked to him, I would only have had to tell him a string of lies. He would find out that his sister was dead about nine that night, of course, when the final editions hit the streets. And I supposed he would instantly come gunning for me when he got the news. But at least I still had a few hours to hope Peggy would turn up.

At five P.M., just as I was getting ready to leave the office, the phone rang again. When I picked it up, Miss Rains' voice said, "It's a woman, Mike, but she won't give her name."

Since it wasn't Sid Trask, I said, "All right. Which line?"

She told me and I punched the proper button. "Macauley speaking," I said.

"Oh, Mike!" a low voice said in my ear. "I'm so glad you're not dead."

I stiffened in my chair. The voice was Peggy Coynes'. "Where are you?" I asked.

"At the Rector Hotel, in room three twenty-one. I'm so afraid, Mike. I can't go home. They'd kill me if they found me."

"Who?"

"You know who," she whispered. "They must be hunting for me right now. They can't afford to let me live. Can you come over here, Mike?"

Another trap, I wondered? If it was, I'd welcome it. After all the pushing around I'd taken, there was nothing I'd enjoy so much as a chance to bounce my knuckles off a couple of faces. I needed a little action to work off some of my frustrations.

"I'll be there in twenty minutes," I said.

I never carry a gun, but I have a license to. For this occasion I broke my usual rule. My short-barrelled Detective Special was in its holster in my bottom desk drawer. Pulling off my belt, I threaded it through the holster loop so that it lay on my right hip, and tightened the belt again. I checked the load, slid the gun in and out of the holster a couple of times, and was ready to go.

The Rector Hotel was a third-rate place on Pernod, in the heart of the slum area. It wasn't exactly a flophouse, but it was the next thing to one. I walked into a grubby lobby where two aged and seedily-dressed men sat on a lumpy sofa sharing a newspaper. No one was behind the desk, but a bell was on the counter for the convenience of anyone wanting a room. Through the open door of the single elevator cage I could see the operator asleep on his stool.

I didn't bother either the desk clerk or the elevator operator, preferring to arrive at Peggy's room with as little advance notice as possible. I took the stairs for three flights.

The door to room three twenty-one was closed. I approached it silently, put my ear to it and listened for a time. When I heard no sound from within, I rapped softly.

Immediately Peggy's frightened voice said, "Who is it?" It came from just the other side of the door, suggesting that she too had been standing there listening.

"Mike," I said.

She emitted a sigh of relief. I heard a key turn, then the rattle of a door chain being released. When she swung open the door, I noted she wore the same dress she had the previous evening. Apparently she hadn't been back to her apartment.

As I entered the room, she attempted to greet me by flinging her arms about my neck. I jolted her away by placing the palm of my left hand between her firm breasts and shoving, causing her to stagger halfway across the floor. Simultaneously my right hand was flashing toward my hip. I spun, kicking the door shut as I did, my revolver pointed at the wall behind it.

That's all there was to cover. Just wall.

After a quick glance around the rest of the barren room, I moved to the closet, jerked open the door and looked inside. There was nowhere else to look. The Rector wasn't the kind of place where you could get a room with bath. There was a cracked washbowl in one corner. For a shower you had to walk down the hall.

Peggy was looking at me wide-eyed. "What did you expect, Mike?"

I put away my gun, walked over and locked the door. I said dryly, "The last time I walked through a door when you were around, I got clouted in back of the head. It may be overly suspicious of me, but I had a faint idea that you were the clouter."

She looked completely stunned. "You thought I hit you, Mike? You think I betrayed you to Tupper Smith." She started to cry. "You came here thinking I'd set a trap for you, didn't you?"

Feminine tears upset me. I had come to the hotel expecting a trap, and determined to ask Peggy some definite questions and get some definite answers even if I didn't find one. I meant to keep it official, and I meant to be tough. It's hard to be either with a weeping woman.

I said uncomfortably, "Cut that out now. There's nothing to cry about."

She only wept harder. "You think everything I told you was a lie," she said between tears. "Here I've been locked in this room, afraid for my life and not knowing whether you were alive or dead. And all the time I was worrying about you, you were thinking I had betrayed you."

I said defensively, "What was I supposed to think? You were right behind me when I got clouted. When I woke up I discovered you'd run off in my car and left me there."

"I had to run," she sniffled. "He'd have killed me, because he knew I saw his face. Oh, Mike, don't you know I'd never do anything to hurt you?"

A man can stand only so many tears. Aside from her own word, I didn't have any more evidence of her innocence now than when I had entered the room. Yet I found myself taking her in my arms and rhythmically patting her shoulder.

"Of course I know it, baby," I said. "Stop your crying now so we can talk. I have to know what happened."

She leaned against my chest and cried quite a bit more before she was ready to quit. Finally she pushed away from me, dried her eyes with a tiny handkerchief and blew her nose. Walking over to the dresser, she examined herself in the spotted mirror and a look of horror crossed her face. She took a compact from her bag lying on the dresser and repaired her makeup before turning around to face me again.

When she finally did turn around, she had completely recovered. In a cool voice she said, "There wasn't anything in today's paper about whatever happened at the cottage last night. I expected to read that Gladys was dead."

"She is," I told her. "I had the lid put on it until the final editions this evening."

Peggy turned white. "They did kill her then. Oh, the poor girl!"

I said, "If you ran from the cottage right after I was hit, how did you know she was dead?"

"I didn't *know*, Mike. I just guessed it. I knew they'd found her when I saw who hit you. And I knew they would kill her if they found her."

"Just exactly what happened after I went down for the count?" I asked.

She shuddered. "He was standing behind the door. I don't think he knew I was behind you until after he hit you. He used a little black sap. I turned and ran the instant you fell. I was all the way down the stairs before he reacted and started after me. I'd have been lost if you hadn't left your car keys in the ignition. I jumped in the car, backed it out of the car port and backed the full two hundred yards to the highway at full speed. I couldn't take time to turn around because he was running down the dirt road after me, shooting a pistol at the tires. He didn't stop until I was nearly to the highway and had left him a full hundred yards behind. He took careful aim just as I backed around the corner onto the highway and fired one last time. But I guess he wasn't much of a shot. Altogether I think he fired five times without hitting anything."

I said, "Who was he?"

"Sheriff Merz," she said. "Tupper Smith was in the cottage too. I caught a glimpse of him looking out the kitchen window as I backed down the dirt road."

chapter twenty-six

I FELT A SURGE OF ELATION at her last words, for they gave me, finally, the thing I had been vainly trying to find for months: concrete, jury-acceptable evidence. With Peggy's testimony placing Sheriff Merz and Tupper Smith at the scene of the crime, with her further testimony both tying the call-girl racket to them and naming Gladys Allerup as a call girl who wanted to quit, I could weave an airtight case of circumstantial evidence even if we never got confessions.

Then another thought dampened my elation a trifle. The murder had been committed in Black County, which meant the warrants for arrest would have to be issued from there, and the Black County District Attorney would handle the prosecution. My only part in the windup of the affair would be to dump the evidence of a cinch case in another prosecutor's lap, then stand on the sidelines and watch him get convictions. The ring would be smashed, of course, but after my months of work I would have liked the satisfaction of personally putting the ringleaders behind bars.

There was another dampening thought too. Unless Merz

and Smith could be made to talk, the real head of the ring would still go free; the big boss, whom I was now convinced was my own chief, Sunshine Sever.

I decided to do a little more thinking before turning my evidence and my witness over to the Black County District Attorney's office.

I said to Peggy, "It was you who phoned in the anonymous tip about trouble at the cottage, wasn't it?"

"Yes," she said. "I didn't know what else to do. I hoped that if they got there in time, they might save your life."

"They know it was you who phoned," I told her with a grin.

She looked surprised. "How?"

I told her of the frame I had found myself in when I awoke from my blow on the head, and how I had managed to destroy all evidence of the frame before the police arrived. "I had to explain my presence there, and I had to explain how I got there when there was no car outside. So I told them I had arrived with you, went inside alone and found Glady's body, then sent you to phone the sheriff's office and afterward to go into town and break the news of Glady's death to her brother."

She looked a little relieved. "Then all I have to do is tell the same story if I'm questioned?"

I shook my head. "Things are changed now. We'll tell the straight story, including about the framed evidence. Deputy Gerard may be a little sore at my coverup, but handing him the real killers ought to pacify him." Then I remembered something. "Why'd you phone both the sheriff and the state police, Peggy?"

Peggy raised her eyebrows. "I didn't, Mike. Just the sheriff's office in Titusgrove. It scared me to death to stop long enough even for that. I thought Sheriff Merz and Tupper Smith might be coming after me in a car, and might catch up when I stopped to phone. As soon as I hung up, I drove the rest of the way home at eighty miles an hour."

I puzzled this over. So it had been some other woman who had tipped off the state police. Alice Dill, I wondered? Perhaps Smith and Merz had forced her to make the anonymous call. The thought cheered me a little, because it indicated that she might still be alive.

"We're going to do things differently with you than we did with Gladys," I said. "I'm not going to hide you out and take a chance on your being found. You're going to stick with me every minute of the time until I put you before a grand jury. You're going to sleep at my place, eat your meals with me and even go to the office with me when I go to work. Even when you're asleep, you're going to be within reaching distance."

Peggy turned a rosy color. "All right, Mike," she said in a low voice. "Anything you say."

"You want to stop by your flat to pick up anything?"

Her eyes widened. "They might be waiting for me there, Mike."

I gave her a wolfish grin. "I hope they are. It would save the state a trial."

She blinked, then rushed to me and put her head against my chest. "Oh, Mike, I'm so glad you came. I'm not afraid at all any more."

I touched her hair with my lips. "I won't let anything happen to you, Peggy. Believe me."

"It's so good to feel safe again," she whispered into my chest. "You don't know how terrified I've been, Mike. Every time I heard footsteps in the hall, I thought they had found me. When I ordered food sent up, I went through agony when the knock came, wondering if it was just the bellboy, or somebody coming to kill me."

"Stop thinking about it," I said. "It's all over. If anybody gets to you now, he's going to have to walk through a screen of lead. Do you need anything from your flat?"

She shook her head. "My overnight bag's still in the trunk of your car. I was so upset by the time I parked in front of your place, I ran off and forgot it. I took a taxi straight here, registered under an assumed name and haven't been out of the room since except to go down the hall for a shower."

I tilted up her chin, gave her a light kiss and released her. Glancing at my watch, I saw it was nearly six. "You paid up downstairs?" I asked.

"Yes. They made me pay in advance because I didn't have any luggage."

"Then check out by phone and we'll leave."

While Peggy was phoning, I walked to the windows and looked down into the street. The room faced the front of the hotel, and my car was parked just below it on the opposite side of the street. I swept my gaze in both directions, not expecting to see any evidence of danger, but merely through instinctive alertness.

My eyes narrowed when I saw a black sedan with two occupants in the front seat parked a quarter-block behind my car.

The sedan was too far away to make out the faces of the two men in it. Probably they were entirely innocuous. On the other hand it was possible that some of Tupper Smith's men had been keeping me under surveillance, hoping that I'd lead them to Peggy.

Peggy was hanging up the phone when I turned away from the window. "I'm ready," she said. "I don't have any luggage except my purse."

"Stand to one side of the door until I check the hall," I told her.

She looked surprised, but she obediently moved to one side. I unlocked the door, then lifted my Panama from the bed where I had dropped it, drew my Detective Special and let the hat fall over my gun hand. Suddenly jerking open the door, I leaped into the hall and spun to cover both sides of the door. Maybe I was being a little melodramatic, but I'd already had one unfortunate experience walking through a door in the normal manner, and I was taking no more chances.

It didn't make me feel in the least foolish to discover it had been an unnecessary precaution.

The hall was vacant except for a woman a few rooms up just keying open her door. She gave me a startled look and I smiled at her. She smiled tentatively in return, and paused with her door half open. She was a dishwater blonde of about thirty, lushly built, but with the flashy dress, hard face and too-heavy makeup of a hustler.

I said, "Okay," and Peggy stepped into the hall.

The dishwater blonde went into her room and slammed the door. Peggy jumped as though she were shot. I grinned at her, put on my hat and slipepd my gun under my coat.

"We won't bother with the elevator," I said. "We'll take the stairs down."

The same two old men were still sitting in the dingy lobby. The desk was still vacant and the elevator operator was still asleep. When Peggy started toward the front door, I grabbed her arm and steered her past the stairs into a hall leading toward the service entrance. The service entrance gave onto an alley behind the hotel.

We turned left and walked a half-block along the alley to the north side street. Another left turn took us to the corner of the street on which the hotel fronted. A quarter-block away, on the opposite side of the street, the black sedan was parked with its rear to us .

I escorted Peggy across the street and along the side street for a few doors after we crossed. When we came to a shoe store, closed for the day, I led her into the recessed doorway.

"Wait here," I said. "I'll be back in a minute."

She looked puzzled and a little frightened at being left alone, even momentarily, but she nodded obediently.

I walked back to the corner and approached the black sedan from the rear. Six feet behind it I paused and studied the two men in the front seat. Both had their attention fixed forward, seemingly on the front door of the Rector Hotel.

I could only get a half profile view of their faces, but it was enough for me to recognize both. The driver was Matty Grange, Tupper Smith's handyman-chauffeur, and his companion was the western-style deputy, Gordy.

Apparently I *had* been under surveillance in the hope that I'd lead them to Peggy Coynes.

chapter twenty-seven

I GLANCED UP AND DOWN the street. There were a few pedestrians in sight, but none closer than a half block away and none, at the moment, walking in my direction. As the street along here on both sides was lined with small shops, all closed for the day, there was little chance of observation from any of the buildings. The attention of the two men in the sedan was too concentrated on the hotel entrance for them to be aware of anything going on behind them.

I drifted behind the car and crouched so that I couldn't be spotted in the rear-view mirror. Snapping open my pocket knife, I drove it into the sidewall of the right rear tire and pushed the blade downward to leave a four-inch gash. As the air left it with a prolonged wheeze, I gave the left rear tire a similar gash.

The rear of the sedan abruptly settled as I walked along its left side toward the front. Flat-faced Matty Grange, in the driver's seat, gave me a startled look as I passed the open car window, and I threw him a chummy smile in return. Both men sat there with their mouths open as I leaned and slashed the left front tire. I had moved to the curb and made a four-inch gash in the fourth tire before either man recovered enough to react. Then both front doors swung open and a man spilled from either side.

Snapping my knife shut, I closed my fist around it to act as ballast, took one step forward and smashed Gordy in the jaw just as his feet touched the sidewalk. The blow drove him back into the car, where he landed flat on his back on the seat.

I stepped toward the front of the car just as the oversized Matty Grange rushed around the hood from the far side. We met at the curb. He threw a wild, looping right at my head, I ducked under it, straightened him with a light left jab to the nose, then put the full weight of my body into a smashing right cross that landed in precisely the same spot I had hit him the other night.

It didn't spin him around this time. It just put him flat on the seat of his pants in the gutter, where he sat with a dazed look on his face.

I threw a quick glance in both directions. No one seemed to have noticed the disturbance. Dropping my knife into my pocket, I walked rapidly, but without undue haste to my own car. I glanced back as I slipped under the wheel and noted that Matty Grange had gotten to his feet, but was swaying and supporting himself on a fender. The deputy Gordy had sat up too, and was tenderly feeling his jaw.

I pulled out of my parking place, circled the block and halted opposite the recessed doorway where I had left Peggy. Her gaze jumped toward me when I gave a light tap on the horn, then she looked relieved. I swung the door open as she hurried across the walk to climb into the car.

As we crossed the intersection, I glanced right toward the black sedan. Both men were standing on the sidewalk, hands on hips, staring at their four ruined tires. Their lips were moving in what was undoubtedly language unfit for sensitive ears.

Examining my expression, Peggy asked, "What's so funny?"

"A couple of Tupper Smith's boys tailed me to the hotel," I said. "Matty Grange and a deputy sheriff named Gordy something-or-other. I spotted their car from your room window, but I didn't want to scare you by mentioning it."

Fearfully she looked over her shoulder through the rear window. "Are you sure they didn't see you pick up your car, Mike?"

"I'm sure they did," I told her. "But don't let it worry you. They can't tail us on four flat tires." I told her what had happened.

It was an indication of how much better she felt, knowing that I wasn't going to let her out of my sight, that instead of being frightened, she thought it was funny.

By the time we had stopped at a restaurant and had some dinner, it was seven P.M. It would be another two hours before the final editions hit the street and I would have a raging Sid Trask to contend with. I decided to get an advance look at the story before he had a chance to see it.

I drove over to the *Chronicle* office and took Peggy inside with me to the composing room. Jim Fusco, the night-trick composing-room chief was an old friend of mine. His ugly face split in a wide smile and he held out an ink-stained hand the size of a waffle griddle when he saw me.

After introducing Peggy I asked him for a look at whatever final-edition pages had so far been run off.

"What some people won't do to save a nickel," he said. "Figuring gasoline for the drive over here, think you'll come out much ahead?"

"Just show us the tear sheets," I told him. "We'll read the funny paper if we want humor."

He led us over to a long table where one copy of each sheet was laid out individually.

"It's all off the press except the front page," Fusco said. "The type's all set for that, but we hold off running it until deadline, in case we get a last-minute flash that Martians have landed in New York, or the D.A.'s office has finally convicted somebody."

He went back to work and left us to our own devices.

We found the item we wanted immediately. It had gotten second-page treatment, and Deputy Mort Gerard had kept his word. There was no suggestion that Gladys Allerup's death had anything to do with the call-girl racket.

The item was headlined: WOMAN FOUND DEAD UNDER MYSTERIOUS CIRCUMSTANCES, and the text read:

The nude body of a young woman identified as Mrs. Gladys Allerup was discovered in an isolated Missouri River cottage by sheriff's deputies and state police at about nine last night. The cottage, owned by Mrs. Allerup's recently deceased husband, is located just off Rivershore Drive between Titusgrove and Clement. Anonymous tips phoned by a woman to both the sheriff's office and the state police brought both to the scene within a short time of each other.

Dr. C. B. Harmon, Black County Coroner, issued a certificate of death by homicide. The victim had been strangled. There was no sign of a struggle in the cottage and no evidence of criminal assault on the victim before she was strangled.

It was learned by police that Mrs. Allerup and a female companion named Miss Alice Dill had been living at the cottage since the death, only a few days ago, of the victim's husband. Miss Dill has disappeared and a state-wide alarm is out for her.

Sergeant Harry Allerup, the victim's deceased husband, was the victim of a similar mysterious and unsolved crime less than a week ago. As reported in the CHRONICLE at the time, he was found beaten to death in the basement of his own flat at 1320 Gaylor Street.

Police tentatively theorize that the policeman was murdered by some criminal gang he was investigating, and that his widow's murder may have been committed by the same gang. It is thought that because Mrs. Allerup discovered her husband's body, members of the gang may have feared she could give some evidence against them.

It is feared by police that the victim's companion, Miss Alice Dill, was either abducted by the killers or murdered in some other spot.

There were a few more paragraphs describing what the

Black County Sheriff's Department in co-operation with
the state police was doing to solve the crime, but it was
all routine stuff designed to assure the public that they
were working. The whole thing had been carefully worded
so as to lull the call-girl ring into believing it wasn't
suspected.

I knew its effect on Sid Trask would be far from lulling,
however.

I thanked Jim Fusco and we left. I drove over to my
apartment house, circled the block twice to make sure it
wasn't staked out, and finally parked in the alley. I took
Peggy in the back way and up to my flat.

While Peggy unpacked her overnight bag and usurped
one of my dresser drawers for her things, I mixed us a
couple of drinks in the kitchen. We sat in the front room
sipping them, both of us quiet for a long time. I was thinking, and Peggy remained quiet so as not to disturb my
thoughts.

The more I thought about it, the less I liked the idea of
turning over all the evidence I had to the Black County
District Attorney. It wasn't professional jealousy, or resentment at seeing another prosecutor reap the benefit of
all my hard work. It was just that my clash with the call-
girl ring had become a personal fight, and I wanted to finish
it on my own terms.

I thought back to the brutal beating of Gladys Allerup—
Gloria Townsend then. I thought of Harry Allerup's in-
humanly broken body, the work of killers who were little
more than animals, and the rage I had felt at that moment
began to rise in me again. I thought of the brutal strangling
of Gladys, and the attempt to frame it on me.

But I think the thing that decided me was the knowledge
that the gang wanted to kill Peggy. All at once I knew I
wasn't going to turn them over to another county to
prosecute. I was going to get them on the Allerup kill—
which was in my own jurisdiction—as well as on the murder of his wife, so that I could smash the ring personally
instead of having to turn the job over to an outsider. I was
going to break the Allerup case even if I had to stand
Sheriff Merz and Tupper Smith separately against a wall
and beat the truth out of them.

Peggy said, "What are you thinking about, Mike? Your
face is as black as death."

"I was thinking about death," I said. "Death for some

people who deserve it. It may be tonight. I'm tired of going through proper channels and getting nowhere. I'm in the mood to go out to Smith's farm and clean house."

Peggy looked frightened. "Not alone, Mike. They'd kill you."

The phone rang at that moment and I glanced at my watch. It was only eight-thirty, too early for Sid Trask to have the bad news yet. Rising, I crossed the room to answer it.

When I said, "Hello," Sergeant Johnny Sullivan's voice said, "Mike?"

"Yeah," I said. "How are you, Johnny?"

"Not so good," he said gloomily. "I think we missed your girl by a hair. One of my boys hit the Rector Hotel at seven P.M., and found that a woman answering her description checked out at six. She was registered as Jane Smith and had no baggage."

In the excitement of finding Peggy, I had forgotten all about the local pickup order I had put out on her. I said, "Cripes, I'm sorry, Johnny. I should have phoned you. You can call your dogs off.

"Oh, you found her yourself?"

I wasn't anxious to have anybody, even as old and reliable a friend as Johnny Sullivan, know that Peggy was in my personal custody. While I felt entirely capable of protecting her, why ask for trouble? "I know where she is," I said cautiously. "Just call the boys off."

"Okay, Mike," he said in a cheerful voice. "See you around."

The next phone call should be from Sid Trask, I thought as I hung up. If he caught the final edition as soon as it hit the street at nine, I should be hearing from him within another forty-five minutes. If he wasn't in the habit of reading the final edition, I still expected to hear from him by ten at the latest. Knowing people, I knew some friend was bound to see the item and immediately phone condolences. Which would send Sid out to buy a paper if he didn't already have one.

Earlier I had been looking forward with marked lack of enthusiasm to the maniacal rage I knew the news of his sister's death would bring on. It presented a difficult problem because I had nothing against Trask. Yet if he came after me with a gun, I'd have to shoot back in self defense.

Even if he just roared over to my flat with the intention of beating me up, it would mean the useless expenditure of a lot of energy for both of us. Energy which could better be directed another way.

That was earlier, though. Now that I had decided to cut through official red tape and take direct action, I welcomed the prospect of his going berserk. I saw a way to make use of his enraged fury.

Walking into the kitchen, I opened the refrigerator and loooked in the meat compartment. I was pleased to find half a dozen hot-dogs. I wrapped one in waxed paper, dropped it into my pocket and returned to the front room.

"Come on," I said to Peggy. "We're going for a short ride."

She rose, looked at me questioningly, but I only steered her toward the back door. A few moments later we drove from the mouth of the alley and I turned right.

The office of Dr. Floyd Hammerskill, who had a quasi-official position with the police department as a poison analyst, was only ten minutes from my place. His office hours were on, but we by-passed the reception room by going around to his rear door and knocking. He looked surprised when he opened the door and saw me and Peggy standing in the alley. He was a tall, stoop-shouldered man of about sixty with a bushy head of hair and a high fore-head which made him look a bit like Einstein.

"Oh, hello, Mike," he said. "Come on in. I've got a patient, but he's just leaving."

We walked into the room and stood waiting while the doctor wrote out a prescription, gave it to his patient along with some parting medical advice and walked him to the door. When the man had gone, Dr. Hammerskill turned to look at me inquiringly.

I introduced Peggy, then said, "Sorry to bust in like this, Doc. I know you must have a waiting room full of patients. But this is an emergency. Got any chloral hydrate?"

He hiked bushy eyebrows. "Sure, Mike. But I can't hand it out without a prescription."

"This is an emergency, and it's official police business," I said. I pulled the wax-paper-wrapped package from my pocket and unrolled it. "I know this is going to sound like a screwy request, but I want enough chloral hydrate injected into this with a hypodermic syringe to knock out a hundred-pound dog. Not kill him, just put him to sleep for a while."

The doctor pulled at his ear and looked at me curiously. "You say this is official police business?"

"Yes," I said. "Don't worry. I'm not after one of my neighbor's dogs for keeping me awake nights. This is for the canine sentry at a place scheduled for a raid tonight. We don't want him to sound an alert before we move in."

"Oh," he said. "Sure, Mike. I guess I can fix you up."

He took the hotdog, went to a shelf and pulled down a bottle of liquid. After drawing some into a syringe, he looked at me thoughtfully. "I'm no veterinarian, you know," he said. "I should assume that chloral hydrate acts on dogs the same way it acts on humans, but I won't guarantee it. About a hundred pounds, you say?"

When I nodded, he said, "Then I'll give half of what would be a relatively safe but sure knockout does for a two-hundred-pound man. I hope it works, but don't be surprised if it kills the dog. Or doesn't affect him at all."

He inserted the needle deeply into the end of the hotdog and slowly squeezed in the liquid. "There you are," he said, handing it to me. "If it doesn't work and you get the seat of your pants taken out, come back and I'll give you a rabies injection."

"Thanks, Doc," I said, rewrapping the hotdog and putting it back in my pocket.

Outside Peggy asked, "What's chloral hydrate, Mike?"

"What's colloquially known as knockout drops, or a Mickey Finn."

We got back to my apartment house just before nine. Again I circled the block twice to see if I could spot any evidence of a stakeout. Apparently the four slashed tires had discouraged Matty and Gordy from playing tag any more that night, for there was no sign either of the black sedan or any other suspicious car. As by then they had had plenty of time to get new tires put on, I decided I wasn't going to be under surveillance any more that night.

I parked in the alley again and led Peggy in the rear way. By the time I had fixed a pair of drinks and we were settled in the front room, it was five after nine. There was now nothing to do but sit and wait for Sid Trask either to phone or start beating down the door.

The phone rang at exactly nine-thirty. As I rose to answer

it, I knew with a feeling of certainty that this time it would be Sid Trask, and that he had seen the final edition of the paper.

My intuition was right. When I said, "Hello," his answering, "Macauley?" was so guttural with rage as to be almost incoherent, but I still recognized his voice as that of Sid Trask.

I said, "Yeah, Trask. I've been expecting you to call."

"You bastard," he said huskily. "Did you kill her yourself?"

I said, "I don't suppose it would do any good to tell you I know who did kill her, would it?"

"You don't suppose right, you son-of-a-bitch. You're in with them yourself. I should have known better than to trust a lying cop. You're all alike. You got her out there just so you could kill her didn't you? And Alice. Did you kill her too, you bastard?"

"I don't know any more about her than you do," I told him. "She's missing and there's a state-wide alarm out for her."

"Yeah," he said. "What'd you do? Sink her in the river? You better start praying, Macauley."

"Why?"

"Because I'm coming after you. Right now. I'm gonna make you as dead as Gladys."

"Oh?" I asked. "Planning on shooting me?"

His husky voice sank almost to a hiss. "I don't need a gun for a son-of-a-bitch- like you. I'll take you apart with my hands. Piece by piece. I'm going to kill you, Macauley."

That had been easy. He was so full of unreasoning anger, he didn't realize I had deliberately needled him with the question to find out whether or not he planned to come armed. Knowing that he didn't simplify things.

"You couldn't tear the wings off a fly, you muscle-bound moron," I said. "Come on over. I'll be waiting for you."

His only answer was the sound of heavy breathing. His rage had reached the point where he couldn't form words any more. The rasping sound of his breath went on for a full thirty seconds. Then there was a click and the line went dead.

Dropping the receiver on its hook, I said to Peggy, "That was Sid Trask, honey. Time to get moving. He should be here within fifteen minutes."

Her face had paled. "Where are we going, Mike?"

"For a ride," I said laconically.

She didn't ask any questions. She simply rose from her chair and followed me out the back door again. When we were in the car I again turned left up the alley, but this time I turned left at the sidestreet too. Another left turn and a half-block drive, and I parked across the street from my apartment house. I left the motor running.

"Have a cigarette?" I asked.

She took one, I put another in my mouth and lighted both by the dash lighter.

Peggy asked, "Can I ask what we're doing?"

"Waiting for Sid Trask to show," I said.

She didn't ask any more questions. Fifteen minutes passed without conversation. Periodically I could see her pale face by the glow from her cigarette when she took a drag. We had both just flipped the butts away when a car screeched in front of the apartment house and slammed to a stop at the curb.

I waited until he had climbed out of the car. Then I called in a mocking tone, "Over here, if you're looking for me, Trask."

chapter twenty-eight

SID TRASK STOPPED DEAD in his tracks and slowly turned around. It was a dark night because here was no moon, but by the light of a street lamp I could see the expression on his face. It wasn't a sane expression. I've never seen a Malay run amok, but I imagine the look they get on their faces just before they start swinging their wavy-bladed krisses at everyone in sight resembles the one Trask wore.

Stiff-legged, he stepped off the curb. I gave him a cheery wave and said, "Good-bye now. Think you can catch me in that broken-down heap?"

Then I gunned away and left him standing there.

I was doing thirty when I hit the intersection. I held that sedate speed for another block, watching the rear-view mirror as Trask piled into his own car, swung toward the opposite curb, backed and finally managed a U-turn. I was a block and a half ahead by the time he got started. I let him close the gap to a block, then bore down on the gas.

We were both doing sixty by the time we reached Lincoln, and we were still separated by a block. I have a siren on my personal car, though I seldom use it. I used it now, just for a moment, because Lincoln is a stop street.

I swung right at Lincoln to City Hall Sreet, touched the siren again there in order to run a red light when I turned left, and headed for Mark Twain Boulevard. In the rearview mirror I saw Trask run the same red light, narrowly avoiding a crash with another car which was going through on the green.

From there on it was a straight run out Mark Twain to the Hawkins Creek Bridge. We were both doing seventy when we hit the bridge, a pretty hair-raising speed through city traffic. Fortunately Mark Twain is wide enough so that we didn't have to do much weaving from lane to lane. I only had to touch my siren once, and that wasn't to clear traffic. It was because a squad car suddenly appeared going in the opposite direction, and I didn't want it to turn and give chase. I touched the siren button in signal to the cops that it was official business, waved as we went by and hoped I was recognized.

The street lighting along Mark Twain is bright enough so that you can make out the faces of drivers at night, and one of the cops in the squad car must have recognized mine. Apparently they assumed the car following was an official one too, for they didn't swing around to come after us.

Once across Hawkins Creek Bridge and onto Rivershore Drive I began to open up. Trask was driving a Hudson and I only had a Ford, but he didn't have a prayer. My Ford has a special head with oversized pistons and a special carburetor. It will do a hundred and twenty with the accelerator three-quarters of the way down. What it will do all the way down, I don't know. I've never tried it because I don't have a flying license.

I was doing eighty-five by the time we reached the edge of the suburbs, and the Hudson had dropped back half a mile. I kept it at that distance, increasing speed every time he tried to close the gap, easing off whenever he began to get too far behind. Twice my speedometer needle edged past a hundred, sometimes it dropped clear down to fifty.

Traffic was fairly light, and with a double lane to maneuver in, it didn't slow either of us.

Peggy didn't say a word until we reached open country, though I was conscious of her tightening up the two times we touched the hundred-mile-an-hour mark. When farmland began to appear on our left, she asked in a shaky voice, "Why are we doing this, Mike?"

"It's the only way I could get Trask out to Smith's farm," I said. "He's in no mood to listen to anything I have to say. This is the showdown, and I want him in on it, so he'll know beyond doubt who really killed his sister."

We sped on a mile more before she asked, "What do you plan to do out there?"

"Tear the place apart," I said. "Back Smith against a wall and let him swallow teeth until he tells me everything I want to know. And Merz too, if he happens to be there."

We passed the motor court I had seen on two previous trips out this way, the familiar army of billboards and the drive-in theater. Next came the two roadhouses which preceded the Lagoon. We were now within ten miles of Smith's farm, and I really began to open up. The half-mile gap between us and the pursuing car grew steadily as the speedometer needle marched past a hundred, slowly moved to one-twenty and stayed there. Peggy braced her feet, clutched the door handle with one hand and pushed her other stiffly against the seat.

"Are you trying to lose him now?" she asked in a breathless voice.

"Just gaining some time. We'll hope he keeps coming instead of turning around and going back home in discouragement. He should recognize my car when he sees it parked on the shoulder opposite Smith's place. Meantime we'll have a few minutes to get Fang out of the way."

I began to ease up when we sailed past the Lagoon, as it takes some time to drop from the terrific speed at which we were traveling. A half-mile beyond the Lagoon I took my foot off the accelerator altogether and started to let the Ford come to a natural halt. I timed it perfectly, barely having to brake when I finally drifted off onto the shoulder and came to a halt directly across the road from Smith's mailbox.

Peggy let out a long sigh of relief.

"We'll have to move fast," I said, sliding out of the car.

"We don't have more than ten minutes. I estimate five for
Trask to get here, another five for him to figure out where
we went after getting out of the car."

I hurried her across to the lane entrance and halted in
the shadow of the high hedge growing either side of it.
Reaching into my pocket, I brought out the paper-wrapped
hot dog.

"You'll have to take care of Fang," I said. "I don't think
he'd greet me as an old friend. I'll wait here while you walk
up the lane a few yards. Don't go too far for me to get to
you in a hurry in case you run into trouble. Yell if anyone
grabs you."

"All right, Mike," she said with only a slight tremble in
her voice.

She moved off into the darkness. I waited, sweating it out,
hoping the dog would appear as quickly as he had the other
night, and wasn't off touring the area beyond the house. A
million stars glittered brilliantly in the moonless sky, but they
didn't furnish much light. Peering in the direction Peggy had
gone, I couldn't see more than a dozen feet.

Five minutes dragged by reluctantly, protesting their short
lives and trying to delay their inevitable fall into the eternal
abyss of time. The sound of a car approaching at high speed
reached my ears.

Headlights appeared at the top of a rise a quarter-mile
away and swept toward me as I drew back behind the hedge
to avoid their glare. The car roared on past.

He hadn't spotted my parked car, I thought with a sense
of frustration. Then, even as the thought touched me, I heard
the squeal of brakes. Peering around the end of the hedge,
I saw by its red tail lights that the car had pulled off on the
shoulder two hundred yards beyond.

Headlights were coming from both directions, and the
car waited on the shoulder for them to pass. When the road
was finally clear, the Hudson swung in a U-turn and slowly
came back toward me. I drew my head back out of sight to
avoid being caught in the headlights.

The car parked on the shoulder on the opposite side of
the hedge, not three feet from me. The headlights dimmed to
parking lights and I heard a door slam. Then heavy footsteps sounded on the concrete road.

I peeped around the edge of the hedge again in time to see
light silhouette Sid Trask's huge figure as he jerked open the

driver's-side door of my car and the dome light automatically went on. The door slammed shut again and he stood motionless for a moment, only dimly visible in the subdued glow of my parking lights.

He walked around to the far side of the car and stared off toward the river a hundred yards beyond. I hoped he would decide to search that way first in order to give us a little more time.

By now ten minutes had dragged by, and I was beginning to wonder if Peggy had even found the dog yet. Then a soft footfall behind me swung my head over my shoulder, and I saw that she was back.

Her face was pale in the starlight, but her expression was exultant. "He met me almost at once," she whispered. "And he gobbled down the hot dog as though he was starved. It worked, Mike. He's sound asleep and snoring."

Putting a finger to my lips, I motioned her farther along the hedge into deeper shadow. As she obediently faded back, I heard footsteps crossing the road again. I risked another glance around the end of the hedge.

Sid Trask was only four feet away, his face bent close to the roadside mailbox in an attempt to read the name on it by the dim light of the stars. I pulled back my head as he straightened and stared up the lane.

Then footsteps sounded again as he walked toward the break in the hedge marking the entrance to the lane.

chapter twenty-nine

I LET HIM GET PAST ME two paces before moving in behind him without sound and shoving my gun muzzle into his back.

"All right, Trask," I said. "Freeze, or I'll blow your spine through your belly."

I should have taken into account the possibility that his maniacal rage might make him psychotically indifferent to danger. He wanted to get his hands on me so badly that almost certain death couldn't deter him. He spun, knocking the gun aside with an elbow, and drove a fist toward my stomach.

I sucked it in just enough to let the blow whistle past, raised my gun barrel and smashed it down across his forehead.

Sid Trask crashed forward on his face, pushed himself up to hands and knees, collapsed again and lay still for a moment. Then he struggled to his hands and knees again and stayed there with his head hanging. He must have had a head like a rock. That blow would have put any ordinary man out for an hour.

I waited as he wagged his head back and forth like a horse shaking off flies, finally brought it slowly and painfully up and stared at me. His expression was dazed, but it was also full of hatred.

I said, "Can you hear me, Trask?" and brought back the hammer of my gun with a click.

He didn't say anything. He just continued to glare at me.

"I don't want to shoot you," I said. "But I'll blow your head off if you make me. I brought you out here to show you who really killed your sister. Behave yourself, and together we can smash the whole murderous ring. Can you stand on your feet?"

With an effort he made his knees. Blood dripped into one eye from the gash my gun barrel had opened on his forehead, and he wiped it away with a sleeve. Then he pushed himself erect and stood swaying.

"Turn around and walk ahead of me up the lane," I ordered.

He still wasn't in the mood to take orders. Disregarding my gun, he lurched toward me with both hands spread for grabbing.

He didn't leave me any choice. He was still too groggy to do me any damage at the moment, but at the rate he was recovering, I knew he would shake it off before long. Easily side-stepping his groping hands in order to give myself time to lower the cocked hammer gently back into place, I raised the gun again and smashed him on the other side of the forehead. This time he remained motionless when he fell.

Damn his pigheadedness, I thought, glaring down at his recumbent body. I might as well have saved myself and Peggy the hair-raising race out here. Sid Trask wasn't going to be of any use, because he looked as though he was through for the evening.

I motioned Peggy over to me, and she moved up to stare down at the unconscious man.

"I planned to have you go back to the car while I tackled the farmhouse," I said. "But I can't leave you here now. I think Trask is out for a long time, but we can't take the chance. He might come around, and in his fanatical mood, there's no telling what he might do. He's crazy enough to try to kill the first person he saw."

Peggy shuddered. "What do you want me to do, Mike?"

"Come along with me. I'll hide you in one of the outbuildings for safety until I get things under control."

Gun in hand, I cautiously started up the lane. Peggy followed, at first a pace behind, then moving up to my side. In the bare light of the stars her face was tense and strained.

A quarter of the distance to the farmhouse I abruptly halted at the sound of heavy breathing from alongside the lane.

"It's only Fang," Peggy whispered.

Moving in the direction of the sound, I looked down at the sleeping dog. He lay on his side, making a noise like a ruptured vacuum cleaner. It wasn't an unhealthy noise, though. It was just an unusually-loud dog snore. Judging from his peaceful expression, it didn't seem likely he'd suffer any worse aftereffects from his Mickey Finn than a severe hangover.

We moved on again, placing our feet carefully so as to make no noise, until we came in sight of the house. I led Peggy completely around it in the same sort of circuit I had made on my first visit. Again lights were on in all the downstairs rooms, but this time none of the upper windows were lit. The barn door was open and the black sedan was inside. Three other cars were parked in the yard, one of them, I noted with satisfaction, bearing the Sheriff's Department seal.

Another was a yellow convertible identical to the one Alice Dill drove.

"They must have Gladys' friend Alice Dill here," I said in a low voice. "Her car's parked in the yard."

Completing our circuit, we stopped beneath a tree some ten yards from the house. I was considering which of the two outbuildings other than the barn I would hide Peggy in before starting my assault, when a woman appeared at the dining-room window. She gazed pensively out into the darkness. In the lighted room we could see her face clearly. She was a redhead with green eyes.

"They haven't killed her," I said in an exultant voice. "That's Alice Dill looking out the window."

Peggy drew in her breath sharply. "*That* woman is Alice Dill? You had *her* staying with Gladys?"

I glanced at her. "Why not? She's Sid Trask's girl friend."

Peggy emitted a low laugh, one tinged with hysteria. "She's also one of Tupper Smith's call girls. Out here she goes under the name of Candy Till. She's the girl who started Gladys working out here. Me too, for that matter. She not only works as a call girl; she's a sort of recruiter for Tupper Smith."

I stood very still, a mixture of rage and self-recrimination washing over me as this information sank in. Of all the women I could have picked as a companion for Gladys, I had to pick a woman who owed first loyalty to the very man I was trying to protect Gladys from. Then some of the self-recrimination faded when I remembered it had been Sid Trask who insisted on Alice Dill staying with his sister, and that Gladys herself hadn't seemed any more enthusiastic about the choice than I had.

No wonder she hadn't been enthusiastic, I thought, knowing what the girl really was. Obviously Gladys hadn't expected treachery, or she wouldn't have agreed to stay with her brother's redheaded girl friend. Alice's relationship with her brother would have been enough to make Gladys trust her. But after breaking away from the call-girl racket herself, she would be naturally reluctant to share an isolated river cottage with the woman who had originally lured her into prostitution.

A lot of things fell into place with the knowledge that Alice Dill—or Candy Till—was a key employee of Tupper Smith's. It explained how the gang had found Gladys. It explained Gladys's confusion on the occasion that she started to tell me that "we" had always kept the news from Trask that she was a call girl, and I interrupted to ask who "we" was. At the time she had side-stepped the question, but I knew now that she had meant herself and Alice. It explained Gladys's hesitation the time she and I sat outside the redhead's apartment house, waiting for Sid Trask to bring Alice out, and I had asked Gladys what her brother's girl friend did for a living. Gladys had finally said, "Nothing, if you mean work. She has an independent income."

It even explained how an essentially nice girl such as Gladys Trask had gotten mixed up in the racket. I could imagine how a young, easily-impressed girl might be flattered by the attention of the sophisticated Alice Dill, and would envy the redhead's exclusive apartment, expensive clothes and big car. Trusting her because she was her brother's girl friend, Gladys must have been easy prey for the experienced recruiter when Alice dangled the bait of big money for easy work before her.

Peggy Coynes, needing money for a sister in desperate need of an operation, must have been equally easy prey. I wondered how many other basically nice girls the wanton redhead had lured into working for her boss in the same manner.

Alice—or Candy—moved away from the window, and I shook myself back to the present.

"Come on," I said to Peggy, taking her hand and leading her toward a dark building which looked like a storage shed.

There was a metal hasp on the door with a padlock hanging from its staple, but the padlock was open. I slipped it off, led Peggy inside and pulled the door closed behind us. As the building was windowless, it was safe to strike my lighter and hold it aloft.

We were in a combination tool room and storage shed. A bench along one side had a rack of carpentry tools over it. Stacked around the other walls were bushel baskets full of empty fruit jars, bags and boxes of odds and ends, a steamer trunk and a few pieces of broken furniture—everything you might ordinarily find in an attic.

I let the lighter flame flicker out. "You ought to be all right here," I said into the darkness. "You wearing a watch?"

"Yes," she said.

I lifted her hand and pressed my lighter into it. "You can check the time by this occasionally. If I don't come back for you by the end of an hour, you'll have to assume I got fouled up. The keys are in my car. Head for it and get as far away from here as you can."

"All right, Mike," she said nearly inaudibly. In the darkness her hands touched either side of my face and her lips brushed against mine. "Be careful, Mike. Don't let anything happen to you. Ever."

Then I was outside again, leaving the door slightly ajar so that Peggy could see out and be alterted to any approaching danger. Purposefully I headed for the farmhouse.

chapter thirty

I USED THE SAME strategy I had on my initial visit to the farm. I quietly walked up the front porch steps and first checked the front-room windows. The television set was on here, but no one was in the room to watch it.

The dining room had a single occupant when I peered through the window. The red-haired Alice Dill was opening one of two sliding doors in the bottom of an oaken buffet. As I watched, she removed a bottle of whisky, slid the door shut again and went into the kitchen.

Since there had been no lights upstairs, and no one was in either the front room or dining room, presumably everyone in the house was now congregated in the kitchen.

Noiselessly rounding the corner of the porch on the balls of my feet, I reached the kitchen window and crouched before it as I had once before. Again I found that it had an insert screen in its bottom.

Four people sat around the kitchen table. Facing me was Tupper Smith. Going clockwise around the table from him, there was the handyman-chauffeur, Matty Grange, then, with his back to me, Sheriff Merz, and to the sheriff's left sat Alice Dill. Apparently the sheriff was alone tonight, as there was no sign of his deputy Gordy.

It must have been a good night for business, for Alice was the only woman still there. The regular standbys must have all been out on dates.

The three men were drinking beer. Alice had a can of beer before her too, but also a shot glass. An empty whisky bottle, presumably emptied by the redhead, stood in the center of the table. She was wrestling with the plastic seal of the bottle she had just brought from the dining room, and not making much progress. The men all watched her struggles without offering to help.

Finally she pushed the bottle toward Sheriff Merz and said in an alcohol-thickened voice, "Here, Mistsure Muschels. You do it, huh?"

The sheriff grinned at her. "What's in it for me, baby?"

She leaned toward him, hooked a hand behind his thick neck, drew him toward her and kissed him full on the mouth. Settling back in her chair again, she said, "How's 'at? Paid in advance."

Merz drew a pocket knife, fingered it open, then paused. "That was only a down payment, Candy baby. If I open it for you, are we going upstairs after a while?"

She gave him a sleepy smile. "Why not?" she asked, shrugging. "Done it for less lotsa times 'fore I tied up with Tupper."

All three men around the table laughed. Sheriff Merz split the plastic seal with his knife and thumbed loose the cork stopper. I decided it was time to move in.

Still in a crouched position, I moved over in front of the screen door and cautiously pulled it open. I did it slowly, so that the spring didn't creak, moved inside the opening and let the edge of the screen door rest against my left shoulder. Gun in hand, I reached up and slowly twisted the knob of the glass-topped inner door.

Then I rose to full height at the same time I pushed open the door, stepped inside and let the screen door slam closed behind me.

"Hands on top of heads," I ordered crisply. "Fast, before my finger gets itchy."

After one startled look, the three men lost no time in obeying the order. The woman, in the act of pouring a drink, slowly set the bottle down and gazed at me blankly.

"You too," I snapped at her. "Don't give me an excuse. After throwing my star witness and your own friend to the wolves, I'd enjoy putting a slug between your pretty green eyes."

Hurriedly she clasped hands on top of her head.

"On your feet, all of you," I commanded.

Four chairs scraped across the floor as they were awkwardly pushed backward by straightening legs.

"Faces against the wall," I said, indicating the wall opposite the dining-room door with my gun. When they didn't respond fast enough to suit me, I added in a voice like the crack of a whip, "Jump!"

They jostled against each other in their individual attempts to be the first to reach the wall.

I relieved Sheriff Merz of his service revolver first, thrusting it under my belt. Then I shook down Matty Grange, finding a .38 automatic in a shoulder harness under his shirt. Tupper Smith was unarmed and so was Alice Dill, whom I hadn't expected to be.

"All right," I said, "you can drop your arms."

Slowly all four brought their arms to their sides, careful not to make any abrupt movements. I backed to the center of the room.

"You, Sheriff. Turn around and come here. The rest of you keep facing the wall."

Sheriff Merz turned to face me and took a reluctant step forward. His eyes were frightened and his bald head and face were beaded with sweat.

I announcd generally, "The first one of you others who so much as peeks over his shoulder gets a bullet in the back." Then I turned my attention to Merz. "Know why I'm here, Sheriff?" I asked coldly.

His head gave an uneasy shake.

"To find out who killed Harry Allerup. You and Tupper Smith are already washed up for the murder of Gladys Allerup, but that one wasn't in my jurisdiction. I want the pleasure of sending you to the gas chamber personally."

He licked his lips and squeaked, "I don't know what you mean, Macauley."

"I'll spell it out for you then. You must know that a witness saw both you and Smith at the river cottage. She's now in the protective custody of the Black County Sheriff's Department, she's positively identified both of you, and there are murder warrants out for both of you right now. I'd rather have you for the Allerup kill, though. You haven't a thing to lose, because you're going to the gas chamber anyway. So let's have a talk about Allerup."

His face had turned gray. He said in an unsteady voice, "I don't know anything about Allerup. Or about any river cottage either."

I looked at him steadily, letting my feelings show in my face. He backed a step, because he didn't like my expression.

"Come here," I said with no particular intonation.

His feet shuffled forward again as reluctantly as though he were wading through glue.

"I'll ask once again in a nice way," I said. "Only once. Tell me about Allerup."

His lips and his jowls and his soft belly all began to tremble in unison. "I don't know anything," he insisted.

The gun barrel flicked out like a striking snake, slapped alongside his jaw and drove him to his knees. Blood dribbled from the corner of his mouth and he spat out a yellowed lower tooth. As he looked up at me with a terrified expression on his face, I raised the gun again.

"The next one will be square across the mouth," I said. "You'll need a whole new set of teeth."

"No!" he croaked. "Don't hit me again! I'll tell you. It wasn't me. I didn't have a thing to do with it. It was Tupper Smith and Matty Grange. Matty held him while Tupper kicked him to death. You can't get me on that. I didn't even know about it till afterward."

"You son-of-a-bitch," Tupper Smith said thickly. "You yellow-bellied son-of-a-bitch!"

I said in a cold voice, "One more remark from any of you people against the wall brings a bullet in the back."

Looking down at the kneeling sheriff again, I said, "How about the beating at the Lagoon?"

When his only immediate answer was to look up at me piteously and begin to pant, I let my expression turn exasperated and raised the gun again.

"Don't!" he yelled. "Matty and Candy beat her up. Candy went in first and caught her with a judo chop. Then Matty took over. I didn't know about that till afterward either. I swear I didn't!"

A low animal growl came from the throat of Alice Dill. Deliberately cocking my gun, I asked in a pleasant tone, "You feel like making some comment, Candy? Or Alice, if you prefer."

She didn't. She stood very still, and I could see her throat whiten. Gently I eased the hammer back in place.

"Now tell me about the river cottage," I suggested to Sheriff Merz. "Which one of you strangled Gladys Allerup? You or Tupper Smith?"

He was opening his mouth to answer when a gun barrel bored into my back. "Let's change the subject of the conversation, podner," the voice of the deputy Gordy said behind me. "Just open your hand and let your gun fall to the floor."

I stood without movement for the space of fifteen seconds. Then I opened my hand and let the gun fall. Glancing over my shoulder, I saw that there was not only one person behind me, but two. Standing in the doorway from the dining room, a frightened look on her face, was a pretty brunette in her early twenties.

With a feeling of chagrin I realized I had jumped to conclusions about the absence of light upstairs. Some men prefer romance in the dark, and apparently Gordy had been upstairs taking advantage of the prerogative all the male members of the call-girl ring seemed to have: sampling the merchandise when there was no other call for it. He had finished his dallying and come downstairs again just at the wrong moment.

chapter thirty-one

SHERIFF MERZ STRUGGLED to his feet. Tenderly he probed at his damaged mouth. Now that I no longer had the upper hand, his expression changed from one of sniveling fear to rage. Jerking his service revolver from my belt, he raised it over his shoulder with the intention of smashing it into my face.

Meantime the three people facing the wall had turned around. Tupper Smith reached out and plucked the raised gun from the sheriff's hand. Roughly he shoved Merz out of the way.

"I want this guy conscious to answer some questions," he growled.

Merz glared at him and blustered forward to grab at the gun again. Tupper Smith leveled it at the sheriff's stomach and drew back the hammer with a pronounced click.

"Don't push me," he said in an icy voice. "After the way you spilled your guts to Macauley, it wouldn't bother me at all to spill some more of them all over the floor."

Rapidly Merz backed away, his face gray and his hands pushed out in front of him as though he thought they might ward off the expected bullet. Smith gave him a contemptuous look, lowered the hammer of the gun and thrust it into his belt. Then he stooped to pick up mine and slipped it into his hip pocket.

Gordy's gun muzzle still bored into my back. I was hoping no one would remember I still had Matty Grange's .38 automatic in my hip pocket when the flat-faced handyman said, "He's still got a gun, you know," and walked over to relieve me of it.

That decided Gordy to give me a complete shakedown. When he found no more concealed weapons, he pushed me over against the same wall my captives had faced a few moments before, covered me with his gun and looked inquiringly at Tupper Smith. Alice Dill walked unsteadily to the table, poured a shot of whisky and shuddered as it went down.

Smith examined me from narrowed eyes for a moment, then turned to Sheriff Merz. "If Macauley was telling the truth about Black County issuing murder warrants, we're all washed up. We'd better find out for sure fast."

His voice was hardly friendly, but at least it was no longer hostile, and the sheriff's pallor disappeared. "Let me ask him in the same way he asked me questions," he suggested in a tone indicating he and Smith were partners again. He held out his hand for his gun.

Tupper Smith ignored it. He looked me over again, thoughtfully, and asked, "Who is this witness you mentioned, Macauley?"

"You ought to know," I told him. "You looked out the kitchen window and saw her at the same time she saw you."

He nodded as though the answer satisfied him. "Penny Coynes. A little tramp who's supposed to be working for me. If Black County has warrants out for us, why'd you bother to come storming out here alone? Why not let the cops serve them?"

"Because I wanted you on the Allerup kill. I can't try crimes committed in Black County."

He shook his head slowly. "That doesn't make sense, Macauley. If Penny was in the custody of the Black County Sheriff's Department, they'd be here with their warrants by now. She knows where the place is. I think you were running a bluff. I think she's skipped town and you don't know where she is any more than we do."

I merely shrugged.

Smith turned to the sheriff. "There's a way to find out in a hurry. You know the sheriff of Black County?"

Merz nodded. "We're both members of the Sheriff's Association."

"Then call him up and find out."

Sheriff Merz looked at him blankly.

"I don't mean ask if there's a murder warrant out for you," Smith said impatiently. "Make some excuse for the call and feel him out." He thought for a minute. "Didn't you say there was an all-points bulletin out from Titusgrove on Candy, under her real name of Alice Dill?"

"Yeah," Merz said with dawning understanding. "I suppose I could call and say a woman answering her description was spotted down this way. That would give me an excuse to ask how the investigation on Mrs. Allerup was coming." Then he frowned. "But if there *are* warrants out for you and me, he sure as hell won't tell me about it."

In the same impatient manner Smith said, "You ought to be able to tell by his tone if he thinks he's talking to Gloria's killer. Get on it."

Sheriff Merz glanced at the kitchen wall clock, which registered a quarter to midnight. "The sheriff himself wouldn't be there now," he muttered. "I'll ask for the deputy in charge of the Allerup case."

Walking over to the wall phone, he lifted the receiver and, after a moment's wait, asked the operator for long distance. Tupper Smith stood next to him with his ear bent toward the receiver so that he could hear both sides of the conversation. Gordy continued to cover me with his .38 service revolver, Matty stood to one side with a stupid expression on his face and Alice Dill sat at the table pouring herself another shot. The brunette who had been upstairs with Gordy still stood in the dining-room doorway, watching the goings-on from frightened eyes.

Sheriff Merz spoke in such a subdued tone, I could catch only snatches of his side of the conversation from across the room, and of course I couldn't hear any of what was said by the person he was talking to. I heard a mention of Alice Dill, and once, quite clearly, the question, "How's it going otherwise?" but the rest of it was only a meaningless jumble of words.

I assumed he was talking to Mort Gerard, since he had said he was going to ask for the deputy in charge of the case. I wondered what Gerard's thoughts were in the light of what I had told him about Merz. If there had been any new developments in the case, I was quite certain the deputy wouldn't tell Merz about them.

I was also quite certain the conversation would satisfy Sheriff Merz that my talk of warrants had been a bluff, because Mort Gerard had no idea that Peggy Coynes was an important witness.

I glanced at the clock again, noting that it was now ten to twelve. I had spent perhaps fifteen minutes casing the house through various windows after leaving Peggy in the outbuilding, and had now been inside about a half hour. I hoped no one would get the idea of searching outdoors to see if I'd brought along any help before at least another fifteen minutes had passed, so that Peggy would have a chance to sneak away.

Sheriff Merz hung up the phone, and both he and Tupper Smith came back across the room. The sheriff looked at me gloatingly. "So there's warrants out for me and Smith, huh, Macauley?" he asked in a mocking tone. "How come Titusgrove don't know nothing about them?"

I didn't say anything.

Tupper Smith was examining me with a bemused expression on his face. "You know, a thought just occurred to me, Sheriff. Macauley must have had some kind of contact with Penny, or he wouldn't know we were the ones at the cottage. He even mentioned that she spotted me looking out the kitchen window, which he couldn' possibly know unless he'd talked to her. Maybe he's got her hidden out somewhere like he hid Gloria."

The sheriff thought this over and his eyes began to glow. "Yeah. And if he told us where, we could tie up all the loose ends."

They both looked at me and I shook my head. "Sorry," I said. "Last I heard, she was in the protective custody of the Black County Sheriff's Department."

The sheriff's face began to turn red, but Tupper Smith merely showed his teeth in a cold smile. In a quiet voice he said to the oversized Matty Grange, "Ask Macauley where we can find Penny Coynes, Matty. Keep asking till he tells you."

The deputy Gordy stepped back a pace, still carefully keeping me covered, as Matty shuffled toward me. The big handyman looked at me expressionlessly for a moment, then drove a fist into my stomach.

As I doubled up, he smashed another fist down on the back of my neck, driving me to my knees. He jerked me erect again by the hair, slammed me against the wall and gave me a full-handed slap across the mouth. I felt flesh split against my teeth, and my mouth began to fill with blood.

Matty paused long enough to ask in an indifferent tone, "Where is she?"

I spat the mouthful of blood directly into his face.

The big man staggered backward, wiped a sleeve across his eyes and his features dissolved into a snarl. He was starting back at me when the slam of the screen door brought him to an abrupt halt and turned his head that way. The gaze of everyone in the room simultaneously jumped toward the door.

Sid Trask stood just inside the room, his face dead white and his eyes blazing with fury. Huge lumps, crusted with dried blood, swelled on either side of his forehead like embryo horns. He looked like the incarnation of Satan.

chapter thirty-two

FOR THE SPACE of a full minute there was dead silence in the room. Then Gordy's gun began to waver toward Trask, but immediately centered on me again when he saw my muscles begin to tense. The slow-moving Matty Grange was the next one to react. His hand shot inside his shirt, came out again, and he was covering the enormous Sid Trask with his automatic.

The giant's bloodshot eyes swept over the room. A whole series of expressions crossed his face when he saw his red-headed girl friend seated at the table. First amazement, then relief that she was still alive, finally puzzlement when, instead of greeting him with a glad cry, she jumped from her chair and backed away from him.

"Alice," he said in a thick voice. "What you doing here?"

"It's not Alice, Sid," I said, which caused his gaze to jump to me. "It's Candy Till, call girl and girl-recruiter for

Tupper Smith. She's the one who lured your sister into the racket. She's also the one who let Smith know where Gladys was hidden out, so that he could come and kill her. Your lovely red-haired Judas."

Sid Trask's face slowly turned toward Alice again. He studied her expression, and when instead of denial, all he found there was an arrogant admission of my charges, his nostrils flared like those of a bull preparing to charge.

He took a slow step toward her, and Matty warned loudly, "Hold it right there, mister!"

Trask ignored him, and everyone else in the room except Alice. He took another step toward her, and there was such an inevitable sense of doom in his steady advance, the girl's arrogant expression turned to one of terror.

"Shoot him!" she screamed at Matty.

Trask took a third step and Matty fired. The giant halted and momentarily his face turned blank with surprise. Then he reacted as anyone with more brains than Matty possessed might have expected him to react. Because he was more bull than man, he reacted like a wounded bull. He charged the man who had shot him, grabbed him with both enormous hands and lifted him high over his head.

Matty Grange weighed well over two hundred, but Sid Trask lifted him as though he were weightless. The gun went off again, so close to the giant's chest that it left a powder burn. Trask winced, but he didn't even stagger. Then Matty was sailing across the room to crash headfirst into a wall and fall to the floor in an unconscious heap.

Trask whirled and was on Alice in one bound. His big hands clamped around her throat.

Tupper Smith jerked the revolver from his belt and shot him in the back. Up to that point Gordy, though watching the action from the corner of his eye, was still carefully keeping me covered. He must have considered Alice's welfare more important, though, for now he pivoted and fired at Trask too.

Unfortunately for Alice, the bullet in his back from Smith's gun caused the giant to swing his back to the wall, bringing the girl between himself and his tormentors. He completed the maneuver just as Gordy fired. Alice went limp as the bullet crashed into her spine.

Smith fired again, the bullet slamming Trask back against the wall and making him release his grip on the dead girl's throat. He still didn't fall, though, even with four slugs now in him. He just stood there swaying.

Gordy was trying to squeeze off a second shot when I smashed him behind the ear and wrested the gun from his hand as he fell. Tupper Smith's gun went off again and Sid Trask finally toppled to the floor. Smith was swinging his muzzle toward me at the same time I brought up the gun I had wrested from Gordy.

Both guns went off, a fraction of a second apart. My slug caught him square in the heart, killing him instantly and spinning his body as he fell, so that his final, spasmodic squeezing of the trigger sent the slug at a ninety-degree angle away from me.

Sheriff Merz, unarmed, was cowering against the wall. The slug caught him in the center of his fat stomach. His face went blank with shock, he clutched both hands to his belly and slowly slid to a seated position on the floor.

I let my gun muzzle droop as I surveyed the battlefield. Sid Trask lay across the legs of the dead Alice Dill, unconscious, and probably fatally wounded, if not dead. Tupper Smith lay on his face, quite obviously dead. The sheriff clutched his stomach and moaned as blood-flecked bubbles formed on his lips and burst each time he emitted a wheezing gasp of air. He too was finished, I knew, because you don't exhale blood and live.

Matty Grange was still unconscious from his headfirst slam into the wall, and Gordy was just beginning to stir. I put him back to sleep with another rabbit punch and looked at the only undamaged person in the room. The brunette still stood rooted in the dining-room doorway, too terrified even to run away from the shooting.

I was opening my mouth to speak to her when she was suddenly spun aside and a gray-uniformed man with a leveled pistol filled the doorway. Simultaneously the screen door jerked open and another gray-uniformed man leveled a gun from that direction.

In chorus both snapped, "Drop it, mister!"

I let the gun fall from my hand. Looking from one state trooper to the other, I gave them each a wry smile.

"Nice timing, boys," I said. "You missed the fun, but you can help me sort out the bodies."

chapter thirty-three

BY THE TIME I had established my identity and had given a brief résumé of events, a dozen more state cops had trooped into the house. It turned out that the one who had first appeared in the dining-room doorway was in charge of the detail. He was a lean, leather-hard man named Lieutenant Munn.

After a quick examination of the casualties, the lieutenant phoned Ross Memorial Hospital for two ambulances, one to cart off the dead to the morgue, the other to rush the still living to the hospital. To my surprise Sid Trask was in the latter group. It seemed unlikely that he'd live with five bullets in him, but he was still breathing when the ambulances arrived.

So was Sheriff Merz, but he was obviously dying. By the time he was loaded into an ambulance, he was in a coma.

One ambulance rushed off to the hospital with Trask and Merz. The other drove off more leisurely with Tupper Smith and Alice Dill, headed for the county morgue.

We had moved into the dining room in order to give the coroner and the ambulance attendants more room to work in the kitchen. As the last stretcher was carried out the back door, a trooper led Peggy in from outside.

She threw her arms about my neck and said, "Oh, Mike! Thank God they were in time."

"Who?" I asked.

"The state police. I disobeyed you. I couldn't wait the full hour. When you hadn't come back at the end of forty minutes, I sneaked up on the porch and looked in. They had you backed against the wall under a gun. So I ran to the car and drove to the state police barracks."

After such an heroic dash through the night for help, I didn't have the heart to tell her the battle had been all over by the time the marines arrived. It seemed that Lieutenant Munn and his men had already been entering the front door when the shooting started, and she thought it was them doing the shooting.

Patting her on the back, I said, "You did fine, Peggy. You probably saved my life."

Both Matty and Gordy had regained consciousness by the time the coroner arrived. After peeling back their eyelids and examining their eyes, he sourly announced that neither needed hospitalization. Lieutenant Munn was all set to have them carted off to jail when I asked him to hold them at the house instead, long enough to answer a few questions.

"Sure," he said. "But what you want to ask them about? Isn't the whole gang accounted for?"

"Not the top man," I told him. "Tupper Smith was just a front. I want the brains behind the operation."

"Maybe we can find some records around here giving his name," the lieutenant suggested. "We'll try that first, then go to work on Grange and Gordy if nothing turns up."

He issued a few crisp orders, and a team of searchers began taking the place apart. They went at it with the efficiency of experts, missing nothing, yet replacing every item they moved exactly where they found it, so that the search left no disorder behind it. Within fifteen minutes a tall trooper came to tell us he thought he'd found what we wanted on the second floor.

Lieutenant Munn and I followed him upstairs and into a small room fitted out as a den. Bookcases lined both walls and there was a large desk by the window. A ledger lay on top of the desk.

"This is nothing," the trooper said, indicating the ledger. "Just an account book of profit and loss on farm products. The real stuff is in here."

He pulled the center desk drawer all the way out and laid it on top of the desk, its front end even with the front edge of the desk. Its back end went only to the center of the desk.

"See?" he said. "It only takes up half the distance to the back. There's a secret compartment behind it."

He groped into the opening, there was a muted click, and he drew a second drawer from the same opening the first had come. It contained nothing but two heavy ledgers.

The trooper was correct in believing this was what we were looking for. The first ledger contained entries listing referral fees paid by every girl who had ever worked for the ring, which incidentally gave us a record, by date and by the call girl's name, of every liaison Tupper Smith had ever arranged between one of his call girls and a customer.

The second ledger was the payoff book, and there was enough dynamite in it to jail a half dozen public officials plus a couple of dozen less important members of the ring. In addition to payoffs to Sheriff Merz and his deputy Gordy, payments for protection were listed to the county district attorney, a county judge, and to two people in the city. One was Harry Allerup, and the other was entered only as "X." Payments to the latter made the other payoffs look like peanuts.

Unfortunately there was no indication in the ledger as to who "X" was.

There were also numerous entries showing commissions paid to various tavern owners and hotel clerks in the city for referring customers to Tupper Smith, which gave us enough evidence to haul in even the small fry in the ring. I was glad to find that my bartender friend, George Stacy, had told me the truth when he said he didn't get a kickback for his referrals, for his name wasn't included.

I found a piece of newspaper in the den's wastebasket, wrapped both ledgers together in it, sealed the package with some Scotch tape I located in a desk drawer, and then taped a white piece of paper to the package. On the paper I wrote a description of where the books had been found, the date and the time. I signed the statement, then had Lieutenant Munn and the trooper sign it.

I handed the package to the lieutenant. "Stick that in your barracks safe," I said. "It's evidence enough to jail a half dozen important people and get fines for a couple of dozen more."

"How about Mr. X?" he asked.

"We'll have to depend on Matty and Gordy. Unless Sheriff Merz lives, which I doubt. Let's hope one or the other knows something."

But when we went downstairs again to question the two men, this turned out to be a forlorn hope. After twenty minues of intense interrogation in separate rooms, both the lieutenant and I became convinced they were telling the truth, and that neither had the faintest idea as to the identity of the brains behind the call-girl racket. Lieutenant Munn ordered both men carted off to the jail.

I said, "If the sheriff dies, there goes our last hope. Why don't you call the hospital and find out if they know anything yet?"

He nodded and went into the kitchen to phone. He wasn't gone more than two minutes, and when he came back his face was glum.

"D.O.A." he said succinctly.

That was that. With the death of Sheriff Merz, it looked as though all chance of obtaining definite proof against the brains of the call-girl racket was gone.

I asked wearily, "Did you inquire about Trask too?"

Munn nodded. "He's still alive, though nobody knows why. He must have the constitution of a rhinoceros. He's in emergency right now." He pulled at the lobe of his left ear. "Don't you even have a hint as to who this Mr. X is, Macauley?"

"I'm almost sure who it is," I told him. "But I couldn't prove it in a million years. There's still one outside chance of nailing him, though."

"What's that?"

"Bluff," I said. "And I'll have to pull it tonight. He must know Tupper Smith's records don't point to him. It's hardly likely Smith would have used X entries unless Mr. X insisted on it. And once the morning papers break the news that both Smith and Sheriff Merz are dead, he'll know he's in the clear."

I turned to Peggy. "Ready?" I asked. "We've got a long drive back to town."

It was one A.M. when we started back. This time we made it a more leisurely trip, and it took us better than an hour. It was twenty after two when I parked in front of the modest frame cottage on Fairview Drive.

"You wait in the car," I told Peggy. "I shouldn't be long. Either my bluff is going to work fast, or not at all."

"All right, Mike," she said.

My feet sounded loud on the wooden steps as I went up them to the porch. Fairview is a residential street, quiet even in the daytime. At that time of night it was as still as a cemetery.

I rang the bell at intervals for nearly five minutes before I finally heard stirring inside. Then the door opened and Sunshine Sever peered out at me from beneath his bushy gray eyebrows. He was wearing pajamas, robe and worn bedroom slippers, and his hair was tousled from sleep.

"Mike!" he said. "What the devil do you want at this time of night?"

"I've got business," I said. "Important business."

He stepped back to let me in and I walked into the front room. Following, he blinked at me sleepily.

"Don't talk loud," he cautioned. "Martha's asleep. You're lucky your ringing woke me instead of her. If she'd had to answer at this time of night, you'd have landed in the gutter on your ear." He pointed to an easy chair. "Sit down, Mike."

I accepted the seat, and he flopped in the center of the sofa, rested elbows on plump knees and looked at me with an inquiring expression.

"I cracked the call-girl racket wide open tonight," I told him. "The whole setup. I've got airtight evidence enough to convict everybody associated with it, right down to the small fry who referred customers for kickbacks."

The D.A.'s eyes widened and he beamed at me. "Why that's wonderful, Mike. What happened?"

"I didn't take your order to drop the investigation, Sunshine."

"I didn't suppose you would," he said ruefully. "Tell me about it."

"I did what I should have done in the beginning," I said. "I cut through official red tape and violated half the rules in the book. Against your orders I went out of my jurisdiction, I personally made a raid on Tupper Smith's farm without a warrant, and I slapped the truth out of Smith and Merz."

Sunshine's smile faded and he began to look worried. "My God, Mike! There'll be all sorts of kickbacks on that."

I shook my head. "I got hold of Smith's private books. They offer conclusive proof that Smith fronted for the racket, and that Sheriff Merz was selling him protection. I also got confessions on both Harry Allerup's and Mrs. Allerup's murders. Tupper Smith and a stooge of his named Matty Grange killed Allerup. Smith and Sheriff Merz killed Mrs. Allerup. They'll both be too busy trying to stay out of the gas chamber to squawk about violation of their constitutional rights."

The D.A. looked relieved. "It sounds like you made a clean sweep. But one of these days your direct approach to problems is going to get you in trouble, Mike. Good God! Think of the mess you'd be in if you *hadn't* turned up any evidence. Smith could have had you thrown in jail for years."

"But I did turn it up, Sunshine. The only disappointment was that the records didn't name the big boss I mentioned to you. They implicate three of Merz's deputies, the county D.A., a county judge and the dead Harry Allerup. But all payoffs to the brains of the racket are simply entered as to 'X.'"

"That's too bad," he said in a disappointed tone.

"Fortunately both Smith and Merz were eager to talk, though. They both named him."

Sunshine's expression turned delighted again. "That's wonderful, Mike. Who is he? Is he in custody too?"

I looked at him blankly. This wasn't the reaction I expected at all. I said cautiously, "Not yet, but he will be. I knew who he was even before Smith and Merz talked, of course."

"You did? How?"

"I told you I asked Lieutenant Spooner to find out for me who was responsible for sending Harry Allerup to Chicago. He did find out, and I knew that was our man."

"Good work, Mike. Who is it?"

He seemed so sincerely eager to know, I began to have doubts. I said, "I don't think you'd believe me, so I think I'll let someone else tell you. Got a phone book?"

He gave me a puzzled look, then pointed across the room to a small table on which the phone sat. The book was next to the phone.

Crossing the room, I riffled pages until I came to the T's. I moved my finger down the sheet until I located the home phone number of Chief of Detectives Captain Mark Towner. I dialed the number, then motioned Sunshine over to stand next to me and listen to the conversation.

After a half dozen rings a sleepy voice said, "Yes? Towner speaking."

"Mark," I said, "this is Mike Macauley. Sorry to disturb you so late, but it's important. We cracked the call-girl racket wide open tonight."

"You did?" he asked in a suddenly wide-awake voice. "Wonderful, Mike. What's up?"

"I need a final bit of evidence to nail the head of the racket, and I think you've got it. You don't know you've got it, but it's in your head."

"What are you talking about?" he asked in a puzzled voice.

"Remember when you sent Harry Allerup on detached service to Chicago?"

"Yeah."

"I was trying to interview Allerup about the call-girl racket at the time, but somebody was deliberately keeping him out of my way. I figured that person must be the head of the racket. I have the D.A. next to me listening to this, Mark. Tell him who suggested Allerup to you."

"Why, sure, Mike," he said slowly. "It wasn't the Morals Division's turn to furnish a man for detached service, but Stan Spooner called me and said he wouldn't need Allerup for a while, if I had anywhere to send him."

I stood there, the receiver held slightly away from my ear so that Sunshine could hear too, momentarily speechless with surprise. With a sickening sense of awareness at how close I had come to making a fool of myself, I realized that Stan Spooner had never asked the chief of detectives who suggested Allerup for the Chicago trip. He had merely told me the request came from the D.A.'s office to stop me from inquiring further.

Then, belatedly, I recalled another bit of conversation with Lieutenant Spooner which should have tipped me off. Together we had laughed about Sheriff Merz's version of what had happened at his office when, according to the sheriff, he had thrown me out bodily. At the time Spooner had said it was a rumor going around, but when I mentioned it to Sunshine Sever, he hadn't heard the rumor. Thinking about it now, I realized no one else had ever mentioned it to me either.

Spooner must have gotten the story direct from Sheriff Merz.

Captain Towner said, "You still there, Mike?"

"Yeah," I said faintly. "Thanks, Mark. I just wanted Sunshine to hear it with his own ears."

When I hung up, Sunshine stood staring at me from bright eyes. "I'll be damned," he said. "Who would ever have believed Stan Spooner was a crooked cop?"

chapter thirty-four

LIEUTENANT STAN SPOONER's bachelor apartment was on Hempstead, only a few blocks from Alice Dill's. It had never before occurred to me that it was a pretty expensive section for a cop to live in. Now, in the light of what I knew, the location took on significance. Rent alone in this expensive area would probably take half a lieutenant's salary.

When we parked in front of the apartment building, I sat in the car for a moment brooding. What was it that caused a man like Spooner to turn crooked, I wondered? He had once been an honest cop, I knew. Even a dedicated cop.

Essentially the city was clean. Once it had been a syndicate town, wide open to every type of racket and every kind of vice. When the cleanup came, a lot of heads had fallen in the police department. The record of every man in the department had been put under microscopic examination by an angry reform commissioner. Stan Spooner had passed with such flying colors that he was raised from sergeant to lieutenant and made head of the Morals Division.

What had caused the change, I wondered? What pressures or temptations caused a once honest man to turn crooked? Had it just been that the opportunity had never risen before, and that the twist in his nature had always been there? It was an exceptional opportunity, of course. As head of the Morals Division in a freshly-cleaned-up town, Spooner was in a perfect position to organize a call-girl racket. Particularly with the co-operation of a crooked sheriff in the next county.

Perhaps that was the answer, I thought. He had been an honest cop as long as the fruits of dishonesty would only have meant peanuts. But when he had an opportunity to step in on the real gravy, he didn't hesitate to turn his back on everything his badge stood for.

Emitting a sigh, I climbed out of the car. Through the open door I said to Peggy, "This is the honest-to-God last stop tonight. After this we can go home."

"Why bother?" she asked. "It's three A.M. now. We may as well stay up for breakfast."

I leaned in to give her a light kiss, then slammed the door and went up the walk to the front entrance.

Stan Spooner's apartment was on the first floor. I walked down a hall laid with richer carpeting than I have in my front room, found the proper door and pressed the bell. After a wait of thirty seconds I was just reaching out to press it again when the door opened.

Lieutenant Spooner's moonlike face registered surprise when he saw me. "Oh hello, Mike," he said in his reserved way. "Come on in."

He was still dressed, after a fashion. He had on slacks and a sport shirt, open at the throat, and was in his stocking feet. As he led me into an elaborately-furnished front room, he said, "I was just getting ready to climb in the hay. I've been sitting up reading. This a social call?"

I shook my head. "Just thought as head of the Morals Division, you'd be interested to know we cracked the call-girl racket tonight."

"Oh?" he asked with raised eyebrows. He pointed to a chair. "Have a seat, Mike?"

"No thanks," I said. "We got the whole ring, Stan. Tupper Smith and Sheriff Merz are in jail, plus a couple of their strong-arm men. Smith's private records showing protection payoffs are in the hands of the state police, and a lot more arrests will be made in the morning. Including the head of the ring. The mysterious character Harry Allerup referred to as the big boss."

Spooner lifted a brier from a pipe rack containing a selection of pipes. "Ever smoke a pipe, Mike? Like to try one of these?"

I shook my head. "We have Smith and Merz cold for murder. Smith on both Harry Allerup's murder and Mrs. Allerup's, the sheriff just on the latter. They know they haven't got a chance, Stan, so they've been singing their heads off."

"They have?" He lifted the lid of a tobacco humidor, frowned after looking inside. "Excuse me a minute, Mike. I seem to be out of tobacco."

He walked across the room and entered his bedroom. I followed and stood watching him from the door. Pulling open the top drawer of his dresser, he drew out a flat tin of tobacco and began filling his pipe, his back to me.

"Go ahead, Mike," he said. "I can listen while I'm doing this."

"They both named the big boss, Stan." There was a mirror over the dresser and I watched his expression in it. It didn't change.

"Oh?" he said. He set the tobacco tin on top of the dresser, reached in the drawer and brought out a packet of matches. He set fire to the tobacco, shook out the match and dropped it into an ash tray on the dresser. "Who was it?"

"You, Stan," I said quietly.

He stared at me in the dresser mirror and I stared back at his reflection. Thoughtfully he puffed his pipe. He picked up the matches and dropped them back in the open dresser drawer. Then he picked up the tobacco tin and placed it back in the drawer too. His hand shifted sidewise in the drawer, and too late I got it.

My hand was flashing toward my hip when he spun with a .38 Detective Special in his fist and snapped, "Hold it, Mike!"

I let my hand drop to my side. "What good do you think that will do, Stan? The state police know you're Mr. X, Sunshine Sever knows it, and Captain Towner knows it. You haven't got a chance."

"While there's life there's hope," he said tightly. "Turn around."

Slowly I turned around, and a moment later felt my .38 ease from the holster at my hip. "Keep your face to the wall," he said.

There were a series of small sounds behind me as a couple of minutes ticked by. Finally he said, "Okay, Mike, you can turn around now."

I turned to discover he now wore shoes, a suit coat and a Panama hat. A closed Gladstone bag lay on the bed.

"You pack awfully fast," I said, eyeing the bag.

"It was already packed, Mike. I just lifted it from the closet. It's not clothes. It's money. Enough to keep me in style the rest of my life. I suppose you drove over here, didn't you?"

I thought of Peggy sitting in the car. "No. I took a taxi."

He smiled at me. "I don't believe you, Mike. I'll bet you have that special Ford of yours outside. I like a speedy get-away car. Let's go."

Picking up the bag in his left hand, he urged me ahead of him with the gun. At the apartment front door he thrust his gun into his coat pocket and kept me covered through the cloth.

"We may as well leave the lights on," he said. "I won't be paying the bill anyway."

He set down his bag in the hall long enough to pull the door closed behind us. Just before pulling it closed, he took a final look around the front room, regret in his eyes at having to leave all his expensive possessions. Then he picked up the bag again and urged me ahead of him. At the end of the soft-carpeted hall I pushed open the door leading outside.

In a soft tone he ordered me to halt just outside the door while he glanced over the cars parked on the street. His eyes lighted with satisfaction when he saw my Ford at the curb.

"Look, Stan," I said earnestly. "There's a girl with me. She's waiting in the car. She'll only complicate things for you. If you want me for a hostage, okay. But don't involve her. Let's go around back and take your car."

His eyes narrowed. "And have her run to the cops when she gets tired of waiting and suspects something's wrong? Who is it?"

"The blonde you saw me with at the Graham. She isn't in this. She doesn't even know who I stopped to see here."

"I'll bet," he said. "Move along, Mike. I'd like to pay my respects to your girl."

I considered my chances if I jumped him, but he guessed my intention and said sharply, "Don't try it, Mike. You'd be dead before you moved an inch."

I saw that he meant it, and that trying to take him would be suicide. There wasn't anything to do but precede him to the car. He steered me around it, following right at my heels, and to the driver's side. At his low-toned order I slid under the wheel. Simultaneously he slipped into the back seat.

Peggy was dozing, but she snapped awake when the car doors slammed shut. She yawned like a kitten. "Finished finally?"

"Not quite," I said. "We have company in the back seat."

She glanced over her shoulder, recognized our passenger as the man I had introduced her to at the Graham, and said, "Oh hello, Mr. Spooner." Then a quick intake of breath told me she had seen the gun.

"The big boss," I said dryly. "With a suitcase full of money. He wants us to take him some place where he can spend it."

Spooner was still smoking his pipe. He took a final puff, knocked the ashes out the window and dropped it in his pocket. "Head south, Mike," he ordered. "In the general direction of Mexico. Stay within the speed limit until we hit Rivershore Drive."

For the second time that night we headed in the direction of Tupper Smith's farm. When we hit Mark Twain Boulevard I gradually increased the speed, first to thirty-five, then to forty, hoping Spooner wouldn't notice but that some cruising squad car would.

Suddenly he said in an ominous voice. "If we get stopped for speeding, Mike, the first bullet goes into the back of your girl's head."

I dropped back to thirty and kept it there until we had crossed the Hawkins Creek Bridge and were on Rivershore Drive. I would have kept it to thirty there too, as a matter of delaying tactics, if Spooner hadn't said, "The speed limit's forty along here, Mike. Get it there and hold it."

I raised the speed to forty and held it to the edge of the suburbs. As soon as we reached open country, and the end of the forty-mile speed limit, Spooner ordered me to raise it to sixty.

I had to admire his self-control. He must have been sweating out the possibility that I had just been the advance guard, and other police with a warrant for his arrest might be hitting his apartment at any minute. If they knew I had preceded them, and put out an immediate all-points bulletin on my car when they found I wasn't at the apartment, we were in danger of running into a roadblock at any minute. Most fleeing criminals would try to put as much distance as possible between themselves and the starting point. Spooner had balanced the risk of roadblocks against the risk of being stopped for speeding, and had decided the latter was the greater risk.

Peggy whispered to me, "Where is he taking us?"

"He mentioned Mexico," I said in a normal tone which the man in the back seat could hear. "I don't know whether he expects us to accompany him all the way or not."

"I hardly think it would be feasible to try to make it all the way in this car, Mike," Spooner said in his reserved tone. "There's bound to be a pickup order out on it by morning. I don't think I'll risk it for more than a couple of hundred miles, then catch a plane to Mexico City."

There was no threat in his tone, but the meaning behind the words was unmistakable. He couldn't afford to leave two witnesses behind to inform the police from what point he had caught a plane. When he abandoned the car, he meant to abandon it empty. Which meant our bodies would be left lying in a ditch somewhere before he left it.

I didn't expect it to come as soon as it did, though. I had assumed he would want to make time first, and that we'd follow Rivershore Drive clear to the state line. But just short of the Lagoon he ordered me to turn right onto what was little more than a dirt lane. The lane petered out at the riverbank after only a hundred yards, ending in a small clearing containing nothing but a deserted fishing shack.

I parked next to the fishing shack and looked over my shoulder at Spooner inquiringly.

"Cut the engine and your lights," he said. "Leave your parking lights on."

I turned off the ignition and dimmed the lights.

The lieutenant backed from the car, leaving his Gladstone bag on the seat, and ordered me and Peggy out. He forced us to walk ahead of him to the edge of the riverbank. When we turned to face him, I couldn't see the expression on his face because his back was to the dimmed headlights. Their subdued glow touched Peggy's features, though, and I could see that she was making an heroic effort to hide her terror.

"Here's where we part, Mike," Spooner said in a calm voice. "I need your car, and I need your girl as a hostage, at least till I abandon the car. But I don't need you any more." The hammer of his gun clicked back.

I felt cold sweat run from my armpits down the inside of my shirt. "Are you crazy, Stan?" I asked. "So far you're only hooked for procuring. Eighteen months and a fine at the most. Add murder and kidnapping to it, and you're finished."

"I'm finished if I'm caught anyway," he said. Though I couldn't see the expression on his face, I sensed the cold smile there. "They can only stick you in the gas chamber once. If Smith and Merz are talking, they'll tell everything before they're finished. Conspiracy to commit murder brings the same penalty as murder, Mike. As a lawyer you ought to know that. And if my squealing associates haven't already spilled that I ordered Harry Allerup and his wife killed, they will. Believe me, they will. I've questioned enough criminals to know how they start to implicate everybody they can, once they begin to break."

I began to laugh. It wasn't an entirely sane laugh, but it was a definite laugh. Spooner regarded me curiously.

"You damned fool," I said. "Both Smith and Merz are dead. They died without saying a word. I just ran a bluff on you. You *can't* be gotten on anything but procuring."

He thought this over. I could almost read his mind as he considered, first, whether or not to believe me, decided he could, and then considered how this news changed his situation.

Finally he said, "In that case I could stash my money somewhere, go back to my apartment and wait, couldn't I? Take my eighteen months, then enjoy my wealth as a free man instead of a fugitive."

"Of course you could," I said hopefully. "Don't be a sucker, Stan."

"There's only one thing," he said in a gentle voice. "Your bluff was too good, Mike. It made me confess I ordered the murders in front of two witnesses. I really don't have any choice now."

He centered the gun on me. I tensed my muscles to jump him, knowing it was hopeless, yet determined to make the try anyway. Peggy, by my side, held her breath.

Spooner's finger began to whiten on the trigger. Then there was a flash of white leg as one of Peggy's feet came up in a beautiful high chorus kick that snapped the gun out of Spooner's hand and off into the darkness. It was a dancer's kick, the follow-through bringing the knee of her rigidly straight leg to her chest, and her foot clear over her head.

Stan Spooner was still standing there with a foolish look on his face when I landed a right to his jaw that lifted him a foot off the ground. He landed flat on his back and stayed there without moving. Looking down at him, I knew he wasn't going to wake up again until he was safely in jail.

Peggy was shaking uncontrollably. I put my arm about her and she began to giggle. I tightened my grip and gave her a light shake.

"I'm not hysterical, Mike," she gasped. "Scared, but not

hysterical. I was just thinking how I used to hate the acrobatic dancing lessons my mother made me take. I never wanted to be a dancer, but she always said that some day I'd thank her for making me take them. I'm thanking her right now."

chapter thirty-five

Dawn was breaking when we finally got away from Police Headquarters after depositing Lieutenant Stan Spooner in jail. We found a diner and had some breakfast.

"When I suggested at three o'clock in the morning that we might as well stay up till breakfast, I was only fooling," Peggy said. She shuddered. "And if I had known how we were going to spend the intervening time, I never would have mentioned it."

"Eat your breakfast," I told her. "I promise honest-to-goodness, cross my heart and hope to die that I won't take you to visit any more killers until after we've had some sleep."

I used the pay phone at the diner to call Ross Memorial Hospital and inquire about Sid Trask. When I came back to the booth, Peggy asked, "Any news?"

"They think the big lug is going to live," I said. "He hasn't any right to, with five slugs in him, but none hit a vital spot. Lieutenant Munn was right. The guy has the constitution of a rhinoceros."

When we left the diner and climbed into the car, fatigue suddenly hit me. "Do you want me to take you to your place?" I asked. "Or do you want to pick up your overnight bag before you go home?"

She looked at me shyly. "I thought I was still in your protective custody."

I considered this. "I think we have the whole gang rounded up," I said. "But it's possible we missed a killer or two. Maybe we'd better not take any chances for a couple of days at least."

I headed for my apartment. It was strange, but by the time we got there, my fatigue had entirely disappeared.

THE END